The Fairy Tale
of
Peckham Rye Park

Being good isn't just for Christmas

an untold story dreamt up by
MeM Tekari

A CIP catalogue record for this book is available from the British Library.

Front Cover Concept Design

MeM Tekari

Front Cover Design

Johannes Roots

ISBN : 978-1-099-12726-7

Contents

thank you for the inspiration

to every child
that walked, hopped, skipped, jumped and ran past
my shop window
chasing after their wildest of dreams

Claude
I **thank you** *for starting me on my seven-step-journey.*
I will forever be grateful.

"There is no greater agony than bearing an untold story inside you."
Maya Angelou

dedicated

to my mother, *who never allowed the light of hope to extinguish*

to my father, *who proved that dedication and hard work will always prevail*

to my darling wife, *whose belief in me has been as crucial as the breath in my body*
I thank you
for your never-ending positivity and support

conception

This untold story is a fictionalised account.

Some characters and scenes have been created
and altered for dramatic purposes
although most of what you are about to read…

…actually happened.

about the storyteller

There are not many storytellers, that can proudly boast of their inspiration as crediting 'every child that walked, hopped, skipped, jumped and ran past my shop window chasing after their wildest dreams'.

However, that's exactly where MeM Tekari dared to trial his first solo publication.

He patiently revealed small tempting snippets of his story, The Fairy Tale of Peckham Rye Park and measured levels of interest by the smiles from his customers and tweaked his story depending on the wide-eyed stares of children and their gasps of excitement.

This all happened in between the everyday 'boring' chores, whilst they collected their dry-cleaning on the beautiful Bellenden Road, Peckham, London.

– CHAPTER ONE –

'Christmas is coming'

A blistering chilly wind whistled its way amongst the children of Belham Primary School and not a single boy or girl was safe, from its wintry sting. The breeze snaked throughout the playground as it ruthlessly hunted for any child who dared to play happily without having wrapped up in their toasty winter woollies. The cold would only be satisfied once every child's cheeks were tinted with a rosy-red complexion and it had left their small bubble noses frozen, numb and snotty.

However, today, the arctic weather didn't stand a chance. There was a certain buzz of excitement jumping around the playground, protecting the children. Today, was the 1st day of December and the phrase on every child's lips was, 'Christmas is coming!'

– CHAPTER TWO –

'it was right there in front of me'

Different corners of the playground quickly filled with groups of cackling children bustling close together. The shrill of their voices echoed with the ugly tone of unashamed boasts of 'My Christmas Wish Lists'; they spoke of some that had taken all weekend to write and described as being 'as long as my arm' and others which 'took six pages to write out neat and with no crossings out.' The atmosphere amongst the children had become frantic as an exciting piece of news started to spread throughout the playground. It was started by Dexter James as he moved in close to his friends; Ivy, Lukas and Billy.

'It was right there in front of me at the dry-cleaners,' Dexter said, dramatically re-enacting the whole scenario. 'My dad collected his work suit on Saturday afternoon, and I saw it, right in front of me.' Ivy and Lukas gawped at each other with eyes wide open, whilst moving in closer to hear more. Billy huddled nearer to his friends, whilst pretending not to be interested in the story that Dexter was telling.

'I'm just trying to keep warm,' Billy insisted as he pushed between Ivy and Lukas.

'Of course, you are,' Lukas replied with a raised eyebrow of suspicion.

'Sssshhhh you two!' Ivy ordered the two boys beside her. 'Please, tell us again, Dexter.'

'As I was saying,' he continued, 'it was hanging on a high rail behind the dry-cleaner man. He tried to hide it behind a long party dress.'

'Oh! What colour was it?' Ivy asked.

'That's a dumb question. Obviously, it was red and white,' Lukas replied over her shoulder. 'Everyone knows the colour of Santa's outfit.'

'I was actually asking about the party dress,' Ivy explained and turned her back on Lukas.

'I don't know. I wasn't interested in the party dress,' Dexter said. 'Gold glitter, I think. Anyway, I couldn't take my eyes off the Santa suit.' He continued to explain his captivating find at the local dry-cleaners and slowly more and more children gathered around him and listened intently. Each child passed the story back over their shoulder to the next friend behind them and in turn, a ripple of excitement grew like a tidal wave as it washed over the growing crowd.

'What's all this noise about then?' A lone voice effortlessly split an opening through the cluster of children and like a piece of magic, the crack in the crowd lead a clear path directly towards Dexter. The voice belonged to Terry Ruddock; the absolute champion, the outright and undisputed winner of 'Trouble Starter of the Year'. The added fact, he was also known as 'Terror Ruddock' did nothing to hinder his fearful reputation amongst those in his year at school.

Terry looked about the crowd for an answer, but all eyes faced down as those closest around him silently scuttled away from within his reach. Terry the 'Terror' slowly walked into the opened pathway like a tiger looking for his next meal to devour and just like the ferocious animal, Terry's reflexes were lightning fast. His arm shot out from his side and grabbed the closest body within his grasp. Unfortunately for him, but to everybody else's relief, it happened to be little Leon Rogers who had been snared by the scruff of his collar. Terry's fat-fingered grip dragged Leon out of the crowd and held him up like a clumsy rag doll. Quivering, Leon struggled with the unforgiving hold he was now trapped in and found himself balancing on the very tips of his toes whilst he eyeballed the face of 'Terror'. With his lips tightened and his face snarling, Terry slowly growled at Leon.

'I said, what's all the noise about?' Leon answered back, petrified beyond belief.

'Christmas. It's all about Christmas.'

'What about it?' Terry snapped.

'We found out where... where...'

'Don't tell him! He'll ruin it,' a well-disguised voice chimed out a warning from amongst the crowd of children. It was enough to push the 'Champion of Trouble' over the edge and his grip on Leon's shirt collars tightened.

'Where's what?' Terry blew impatiently, barking back.

'We found out where Father Christmas gets his outfit cleaned,' Leon blurted out before raising his trembling hand slowly and pointing his pokey finger at Dexter. 'He told us. It's just across the road from the school, at the dry-cleaners. He said he's even seen it.' Terry's attention swiveled around and traced the direction of Leon's pathetic pointing digit. The entire crowd followed Terry's glare as it moved towards Dexter, who in turn, swallowed hard the very moment he felt all eyes focus upon him.

Terry's intense stare and entire focal point had shifted. He released his vice-like grip from Leon's shirt collar, which in turn, caused him to buckle and instantly drop fast to his knees. However, the embarrassment caused him to scramble straight back up to his feet like a baby lamb taking its first wobbly steps in life. Leon desperately brushed at the dirt from his clothes whilst trying to disguise his hurt pride with a smile. Unfortunately, he was unable to hide the tears from welling up in his eyes and this was the usual ending for anyone who crossed paths with the one and only 'Terror Ruddock'.

Terry had now moved closer towards Dexter, who stood rooted to the spot like a rabbit caught in the headlights of an oncoming car.

'So? Is it true?' Terry huffed, surprisingly in a softer tone than expected.

'Yes, it's true.' Dexter said. Before Terry could ask another question, the crowd of children dispersed at the sudden 'ding-a-ling-ding-dong' ring of the bell that chimed out loud, letting everyone know that playtime had now ended. The children skipped off and headed back into school and straight to their classrooms. The electric excitement from the playground followed them all in and it stuck very close to Dexter as Terry turned and spoke to him.

'I've got an idea about that Father Christmas suit and you're going to help me.'

'Help with what?' Dexter asked.

'We're going to have some fun and find out who Father Christmas really is.' Terry's face was cracked by a sinister grin that revealed his plan. As Dexter stepped back into school, an instant dread filled his body and he was certain that he felt his heart skip a beat. He knew very well; this was not a feeling that would lead to a good idea.

– CHAPTER THREE –

'oh wow! it's true, it really is in there'

Having completed the one o'clock registration, Miss Lawford revealed that they were all about to venture outside of school for their latest afternoon project, which was called, 'The Place Where I Live.' She was left bemused as her announcement caused the entire class to squeal out loud in elation, for she had half expected them to object because of the cold weather. Unbeknown, to Miss Lawford, the children were filled with a buzz of excitement at the chance of walking past the dry-cleaners, not only on their way out but also on their way back to school.

The whole class stood in two rows by the exit gates in the playground. There seemed to be a feeling of 'unfinished business', between Dexter and Terry floating in the air and so everyone steered clear of being partnered with either of them. Miss Lawford delivered the usual strict instructions.

'Outside of these gates, you will always walk and never run. Keep yourselves side by side, never let go of your partner's hand and always follow the person in front. Have I made myself clear Class 2B?'

'Yes Miss Lawford,' the whole of 2B responded. They were on the brink of bursting with hysteria. The class was joined by Miss Goode, another teacher, who would help keep an extra pair of eyes on the caterpillar-like line that squirmed ready to follow their teacher out of the school. Her eagle-eyed glare noticed a break at the back end of the queue of children and she set off to put it right immediately.

'Hey, you two. Dexter, Terry,' her finger pointed out at the two boys as she continued. 'Hold hands please, otherwise, we can't set off,' Miss Goode ordered the two boys at the back of the line. Dexter reluctantly held onto Terry's hand and they instantly became partnered together.

An unexpected hush suddenly engulfed the queueing children as they stepped out through the school gates and made their way over the first crossing. In fact, the quietness was so out of character for the class, it caused Miss Lawford to turn around with concern from the other side of the road.

'Well done class. Well done to you all.' She praised the calmness of the children. The two teachers exchanged eyebrow raising glances at each other as they continued leading their class. They were completely unaware that the children were struck silent by their anticipation at seeing the Father Christmas suit in the dry-cleaners. Once over the road, the children were less than twenty steps away from passing the shop and just like a procession of soldiers on parade, all heads automatically turned left in unison as they neared the front window.

A fantastic stroke of luck had befallen the nearing trail of children as they found the shop's double front doors wedged wide open. The owner walked out with a delivery he was loading into his van at the very same moment; it was the perfect opportunity to look inside the shop.

An awe-inspired gasp fell from the lips of every child as they passed the open doors, and each flabbergasted intake of breath was accompanied by whispered words of confirmation, over their shoulder, to the child following on from behind.

'It's true!' Ivy announced.

'Oh wow, I saw it too,' another voice chirruped.

'I told you. It's red and white.' Lukas said. 'It's hanging at the back, on the left!

'Yes! It's really in there. I saw it.' Leon announced. He directed his acknowledgement over the heads of those behind him, particularly towards Terry. The excitement caused the children to slow down and stumble into each other like a mini traffic jam as they lost all focus of the direction, they were heading in.

'Turn around, Leon! Look where you're going!' Miss Goode bellowed at him.

'Sorry Miss. I got a little distracted,' Leon replied in a sickly saccharine-like tone.

'Just watch where you're going, please,' Miss Goode demanded again.

'Looks like you were telling the truth.' Terry leaned over and snarled at Dexter. The squeals of astonishment continued as the message was passed on and reached the end of the queue. It was now both Terry and Dexter's turn to pass the open door. Terry dropped to one knee and fiddled with his laces, whilst pretending to do them up. His plan had given him valuable extra seconds to catch sight of the wonder everyone else had already briefly witnessed.

'Terry Ruddock! Dexter James! Get a move on and catch up before I pull you two up to the front.' Miss Lawford's patience had been tested and she stated her authority.

The van had been loaded and the dry-cleaner man headed back into his shop.

'Hey, Mr. Dry-Cleaner Man! Is that Father Christmas outfit real?' a needy question fell out of Terry's mouth as he pointed directly at the red and white suit inside the shop.

'Sssshhhh,' the man placed a finger over his pursed lips and paused for a second, 'best we say nothing, I think.' He winked at Terry and Dexter who both felt the raging stare of Miss Goode lock onto them as she approached.

'I'm so sorry about that. They have been told specifically not to disturb any of the businesses on the street,' Miss Goode explained.

'It's no problem. Just kids doing what they do, always asking questions,' the dry-cleaner man said, whilst heading back into the shop.

He paused only to remove the wedges from the double doors and closed them both behind him as he did so.

Although it was close to an hour since the class had passed the dry-cleaners, every child had left their thoughts right outside of the shop. It had become apparent to Miss Lawford and Miss Goode that suddenly none of the children had any interest in their current school project and both teachers were left baffled as to why and what had distracted the entire group so much. However, the children were determined to `keep their find' a secret between themselves and the only thing on their young minds as they returned was to catch a second glimpse of the outfit. The returning parade slowed its pace as it approached and just as they had done earlier, every head in the queue turned like clockwork, to catch another glimpse of the treasured sight.

– CHAPTER FOUR –

'it's true, it has gone'

The next morning, back in the playground, a new rumour had quickly started to circulate between the small huddles of children who had gathered together. The latest tale seemed to leave broken hearts everywhere it was heard.

'I'm sure it was hanging in the same place.' Ivy's best friend, Bella Reese, had an uncertain quality in the tone of her voice as she spoke.

'I couldn't see it,' another voice landed amongst the discussion.

'I looked again into the shop this morning. It's true, it has gone.' There was a slight waver as Ivy spoke which confirmed the group's worst nightmare. And just as they thought it couldn't get any worse, Terry Ruddock crashed in between the girls like a bull in a china shop which took them by surprise.

'What's with all the sad faces, saddo's?' he snorted at them.

Meanwhile, in another corner, amongst another huddle of bodies, a similar conversation was taking place.

'My dad dropped off some shirts this morning and I went inside with him.' Dexter was talking under his breath. Lukas and Billy took turns as a lookout, keeping a sharp eye focused on an unwanted visit from the 'Terror' of the playground. 'I couldn't see it anywhere,' Dexter continued.

'It's too early for it to have been collected already, isn't it?' Lukas questioned.

'Yes, we're still a few weeks away from Christmas,' Billy responded.

'Well, I didn't see it hanging in the same place as yesterday. I have no idea if it's gone or not.' Dexter's claim was met with the sudden thud of a rucksack being hurled into the three-boy crowd like a bowling ball striking a set of pins. Terry pounced in amongst the tight-knit group and gathered his rucksack whilst making his intentions known to them.

'And that's why me and Dexter are going to see the dry-cleaner man.'

'What? Who?' Dexter stepped back to regain his balance. Terry's brash announcement almost knocked Dexter off his feet.

'You heard. After school tonight, me and you. We're going to visit the dry-cleaners.' Terry's words fell from his mouth with a rebellious certainty.

'How am I supposed to do that? My mum picks me up after school.' Dexter tried to explain his way out of his tricky predicament. 'So, that can't happen,' he said. Terry dropped his rucksack to the ground and stepped closer to Dexter. Billy and Lukas simultaneously stepped away in the opposite direction like ballroom dancers moving through a routine.

'Well, it's a good thing that I've got all day to come up with an idea... for us both.'

The thought that 'Terror' Ruddock was plotting a scheme filled Dexter with dread and the notion of it sat in his belly for the rest of the day.

During the art class, Dexter watched Terry staring out of the window for the entire period of the class. He even told Miss Lawford that he was looking for inspiration. During reading time, Terry sat with his brow furrowed, chewing on the tip of his pencil whilst deep in thought and once they took out their books for the 'Where I Live Project', Miss Lawford called upon the class.

'Okay 2B. Come on! Let's play Q and A. So, who's first? Any questions about your neighbourhood?' she asked.

'Ohhh yes!' Terry jolted to his feet. It was as if from nowhere, a hot chunk of inspiration fell into his lap and caused him to bounce out of his seat. He spoke his thoughts aloud with a clenched fist punching the air. 'That's it, questions and answers!'

'I do not expect any shouting out. Sit down and hand up if you want to be heard,' Miss Lawford said.

'I'm sorry Miss. I just had a thought,' Terry said back to her.

'I'm aware it must be a strange sensation, but it doesn't give you the right to shout out in class. So, sit down and enjoy the moment,' she quipped back at Terry. He slumped back down into his seat, crouched over his book and manically scrawled his idea over the blank pages before it had the chance to escape out of his mind. The prospect of Terry's master plan coming together sent a shiver crawling over Dexter's skin.

– CHAPTER FIVE –

'it's a fantastic idea already'

The school day had come to an end and Terry cornered Dexter, Billy and Lukas in the corridor. Terry shoved his way in between the boys and handed over a scrappy piece of paper to Dexter, his new unwitting partner in crime.

'This is it,' Terry looked around as he whispered. 'This is the plan. Tell your mum we have to go to the dry-cleaners tonight.' Dexter looked on puzzled as he listened to Terry's instructions.

'But my dad's clothes won't be ready until the weekend,' Dexter pointed out.

'We're not going there to pick up his dry-cleaning,' Terry huffed. 'We are going as part of our project. It's our homework for tonight.' Terry rolled his eyes before he continued. 'We need to interview a local shop keeper in the area, and so we've chosen the dry-cleaner man.' Terry stepped back and opened his arms. His face was plastered with confidence, whilst his chest was puffed and bursting with pride as he revealed his amazing masterplan. 'We need to be quick on this,' Terry demanded.

'Why is there such a rush? Dexter asked. 'Let's think the plan out overnight; maybe, you'll come up with a better idea tomorrow.' Dexter wanted to steer away from Terry's plan. He felt something very wrong with it and the fact that it would start with him telling his mother a lie was a sure sign of a wrongdoing.

'What do you mean, a better idea tomorrow? It's a fantastic idea already and it has taken me all day to think it up.' Terry took a step closer to Dexter. 'And I won't risk anyone else stealing my idea and seeing the dry-cleaner man before me… or us,' Terry warned his accomplice. 'I'll follow you out to the car, you go on ahead,' Terry ordered. Dexter set off with no choice.

Terry only had the patience to give Dexter a five second head start before following on after him. As he approached the car, he could hear Dexter struggling to deliver his rehearsed lie to his mother as she spoke back through the half-opened car window.

'Hello Mum.'

'Let's be quick please Dexter,' his mother, Anne-Marie said. 'We have to pick up Charlotte from her ballet class. It's been cancelled, last minute again.'

'I need to go to the dry-cleaners, across the road' Dexter started.

'What? Why? What on earth are you dry-cleaning?' she quizzed.

'No nothing. Well, he has a project for us and… Errrrm…'

'Hello, Mrs. James.' The sickly-sweet tone of Terry's voice poured over Dexter's shoulder and through the open window as he moved closer to the car. The look on Anne-Marie's face couldn't help but express her feelings of confusion and frustration, which Terry read well. He instantly adapted himself to the moment he unexpectedly found himself in. 'It's no problem Dexter, we can go tomorrow after school,' Terry leaned into the car. 'I'm working together with Dexter on a school project. We must spend ten minutes interviewing a local shopkeeper. But it's not urgent. If it's okay with you, can we take some time tomorrow after school?'

'Errrrm… yes. After school tomorrow is okay.' Anne-Marie found herself agreeing.

'Thank you, Mrs. James, it's nice to meet you finally.' Dexter looked on stunned at Terry's bizarre performance, but he wasn't finished yet. Terry directed his attention back at Dexter and continued as he opened the back door of the car for his friend, 'Hurry up Dexter, or you'll be late to pick up your sister.'

'Yes, come on Dexter.' Anne-Marie directed over her shoulder at her son. He stepped into the car and slumped down, looking back at Terry who shut the door and was now waving robotically as the car pulled away and drove off.

'Well, he seems to be a very charming boy.' Anne-Marie looked at the reflection in the car mirror as she spoke.

'Yeah, he's the most,' Dexter sighed back at his mother.

– CHAPTER SIX –

'I'm not going to lose this chance to ask for my wish'

The next day at school seemed to just drag for Dexter as he lugged upon his thin shoulders the heavy burden of guilt which felt knotted and awkward to carry.

However, eventually he found himself at the end of the school day and cornered in the corridor by the voice of 'Terror'. He was coaching him on how to expertly deliver a gift-wrapped lie to his mother, who was parked outside ready to pick up her son. Dexter wasn't looking forward to handing over the well-orchestrated fib to his mother.

'Just tell her it's ten minutes of questions for the dry-cleaner man,' Terry directed. 'I'll be straight there to back you up. Anyway, she agreed to it yesterday.'

'I can speak to the dry-cleaner man on Saturday if you like? I'm going there with my dad this weekend.' Dexter tried to casually throw his suggestion into the conversation, but Terry was not having any kind of swaying to his plan.

'This was my idea. I'll speak to the dry-cleaner man myself,' Terry firmly stated.

'But he's quite friendly with my dad.' Dexter tried to explain. Terry placed his hand onto Dexter's shoulder and took a grip, keeping him in place. With a determined glare, he looked Dexter straight in the eyes.

'Well, if I ever get a chance to ask Father Christmas for my wish, maybe when my dad's home, he'll be great friends with the dry-cleaner man too.' Terry had let his guard down, but it was only for a split second. 'I'm not going to lose this chance to ask for my wish.' His grasp on Dexter tightened. It was enough to let him know how decisive he was to see his plan go into action. 'If this doesn't happen, I don't want to blame you.' The threat of Terry's tone clung to Dexter like sticky toffee treacle. He swallowed and gulped back down the fear that filled him and so set off to see his mother outside. Once again, Terry's impatience did not allow him to hang around and he bounded off after his accomplice.

'Oh, hi Mum…' Dexter waved as he approached the car.

'Hello, Mrs. James.' Terry slithered between them both and seamlessly continued. 'My mum said to thank you very much for waiting for us as we interview the dry-cleaner man. It's only ten minutes at the most but she can never make it down here, not with my baby sisters as well.'

'Oh, hello again Terry.' A surprised Anne-Marie responded. 'I've got this parking spot for another ten minutes, so I'll wait here. Good luck with the interview boys.'

'Ohhh yes!' Terry fist pumped the air before turning and grabbing Dexter. 'Okay, this is it, let's do it!'

'Hi you two.' Ivy yelled from the gates as she left school.

'Bye to you!' Terry shouted back over to Ivy. 'We're busy, so you can keep on moving!' Anne-Marie was left startled by the interaction between Terry and the 'nice girl across the road' but shook it off as she mumbled under her breath to Dexter.

'You kids, today.' Dexter smiled an apologetic smile at his mother, shrugging his shoulders before he turned to chase after Terry who had already set off on his mission.

– CHAPTER SEVEN –

'this is The Book of Names'

The boys walked into the dry-cleaners and were immediately comforted by the warm air that circulated around them from the steam that hissed from the back of the shop. On a typical winter's day in December, it was a feeling of pure luxury and the man behind the counter welcomed them both in.

'Hello there, how can I help?' he asked with a smile. Terry stood rooted to the spot as he focused on the Father Christmas suit which was now, thankfully, hanging on a new rail just behind the counter.

'Errrrm… is this the dry-clean shop?' asked Dexter hesitantly. The man turned and looked around the surroundings of the shop before answering.

'Yes, this is the dry-cleaners,' he said. Dexter approached the counter completely oblivious to the twang of sarcasm in the man's response and asked another question.

'What's your name?'

'My name is…'

'No, I mean the name of the shop.' Dexter was quick to correct himself.

'It's Friends of Fabric. Didn't you see it on the sign outside?' The shop keeper pointed as he spoke, but Terry was quick to interject.

'Oh yeah, we know all that, we're just double checking with you that we've got the right place. Can we interview you for our school project please?' Terry asked.

'Will it take long?' came the enquiry, 'as I'm a bit busy at this moment.'

'It's just a couple of questions.' Dexter confirmed.

'Well, you've already asked me two questions and the answers are written outside above the door.' The man recognized the boys' uniform belonging to the school from just across the road. He was good friends with Miss Lawford and so remained quite relaxed and patient with the unexpected 'interviewing process' he found himself subjected to.

'How long have you been here?' Dexter asked.

'Since 2001. Oh, that's written outside on the sign as well,' he apologetically pointed again up towards the shop sign.' His face held the kind of expression that said another question had been wasted. Dexter tried to ignore his slip up and paused. He scratched his head as he thought of another question. He quickly realised that the interview was not going well, so Terry took the initiative and stepped in. His finger thrust out pointing over the counter to the side rail.

'Hey, Mr. Dry-Cleaner Man, who does that Father Christmas outfit belong to?' The man looked at the outfit, paused and took a breath before he spoke.

'Well, you've already answered that question. It belongs to Father Christmas,' he leaned in closer over the counter and spoke in a hushed tone with his finger over his lips. 'Please promise, that you won't reveal it to the other children from your class.' Terry took a sharp breath and questioned again purely for his own satisfaction.

'If it's such a secret why's it hanging there, in full view of everyone passing by?'

'Oh yes! Good question,' Dexter couldn't contain himself, and he had just witnessed Terry ask a super question. This time, the dry-cleaner man leaned in even closer. His voice now just hushed above a whisper.

'Think about it, if I had hidden this in a secret place and it was found, then it would be obvious who it belonged to. But, when I leave it up here in full view, then nobody ever believes me when I tell them who it actually belongs to.' The dry-cleaner man stood back up, tapped his nose with his finger twice and winked at the boys. Terry and Dexter looked at each other and gulped down their thoughts. But Terry couldn't control his curious mind and blurted out yet another question at the man.

'So, when is it going to be picked up?' Terry's tone almost demanded an answer.

'Why arc you so interested in that outfit? I have something, that is ten times, no wait, a hundred... no, possibly a million times more interesting than a Father Christmas outfit.'

'Mr. Dry-Cleaner Man, it's December and...' Terry looked at Dexter and then both boys spoke in perfect unison, 'the most important time of this month is Christmas.'

'Wrong!' the man announced just as a gentle tinkle chimed from the door and a serious looking man, with his brow furrowed, walked into the shop and handed in a ticket. The dry-cleaner man searched along a nearby rail, returned with his order and passed over the item to the customer.

'Here's your coat, sir. All cleaned and paid for, thank you very much.' The customer mumbled his thanks and left still wearing the same intense look as when he had entered. Without missing a beat, the dry-cleaner man pulled out a paper bag from under the counter and unwrapped its contents.

'Young gentlemen, during the month of December, let me present the most important item held within this shop,' he slowly peeled away the plain wrapping to reveal a red book hidden inside.

'A book?' Dexter questioned. The revelation caused Terry to scrunch his nose at the item with little care or any interest.

'Who's going to bother to read that doorstop?' Terry questioned. The tone of his voice was aghast, should he ever be faced with such a task. The dry-cleaner man pointed at the book and gently placed his fingertip upon its front cover.

'This is 'The Book of Names: Deserved and Flip-Reversed' he announced. 'Every deserving child on this side of Peckham which appears in the 'Deserved' section of this book will get a visit on Christmas Eve.'

'And what does 'deserved' mean exactly?' Terry stepped up to the counter and asked as his wide-eyed stare fell on the book. Dexter stood motionless; his eyes fixated on the hidden pages that seemed to hold a mysterious wonder that stopped both the boys in their tracks.

'I think, deep down, most children tend to know if they have been deserving at the end of the year, don't you?' the man asked Terry directly. The question caused twelve months of flashbacks to pass through Terry's mind and he tried to recall all the moments, he had been 'deserving' rather than not. The interview was disturbed by a car horn 'beeping' from outside. Anne-Marie had turned the car around and parked outside Friends of Fabric. She tooted on the horn of the car again and pointed at her watch. Dexter realised his homework interview had overrun.

'Okay thank you for your time, Mr. Dry-Cleaner Man. We have to go now,' he said.

'Wait!' Terry stumped up, 'if it holds the deserving names, then where are the non-deserving, held?'

'Oh, they're written on the flip-reversed side.' The dry-cleaner man said casually, as he turned the book over and into the right direction. 'Those names are on this side,' he continued to flick through. Terry quickly leaned up on to his tiptoes to catch a look at the flip-reversed pages, but the book was shut again and placed under the counter out of sight. The car horn beeped again, which led to both the boys announcing that the interview was now over. The dry-cleaner man watched them return into the bitterly cold afternoon and towards the waiting car outside. Dexter opened the car door and heard his mum have her say.

'Hey, you two said, ten minutes at most. Let's be quick, your sister needs the toilet.' She looked over Dexter's shoulder and called out at Terry.

'Terry! Can we give you a lift?' she asked. 'It's freezing out here, we'll drop you off.'

'Errrrm, no thanks, Mrs. James. You're okay. My brother is coming to pick me up. I have to wait over by the school gates.' Terry's limp hand raised up, half pointed and dropped to his side as he swung his bag over his shoulder. Dexter looked on and watched Terry trudge away off into the opposite direction of the gates. He noticed that something was not quite right with Terry.

– CHAPTER EIGHT –

'everything he has said is true, I was with him'

The next morning the playground was alive again. There had been a delicate sprinkling of snow which had softly settled, but thankfully, it was not enough to cancel playtime outside. However, today's story in the playground was so hot the children in Year Two were convinced that it would melt the flakes to slush. Once again Dexter was at the epicenter of all the interest and noise.

'So, are you saying that you actually saw this book?' asked Ivy.

'How many names did it have in it?' squealed Samuel.

'I helped my gran last week. Did you see my name in it? questioned Olivia.

'Why does the dry-cleaner man have it?' enquired Jack.

Dexter spun amongst the now over excited crowd like the hands of a clock and answered every question precisely in turn.

'Yes, we actually saw the book,' he turned 'we didn't open it to count up the names,' he turned again 'so, no, we didn't see your name,' he turned once again 'he obviously has it because he has the outfit as well... and they belong together.'

'Why should we believe you saw it?' It was a question that immediately dampened the atmosphere as the voice of doubt fell from Steven's lips.

'You can believe it because I was with him,' Terry stood at the back of the crowd. His voice once again opened a pathway between him and Dexter. Terry walked into the circle and stood beside Dexter. 'Everything he has said is true. I was with him.' Discreet gasps of excitement hissed in the air around the boys as the crowd demanded to hear more about the revelation. However, the end-of-break-bell echoed out loudly as it chimed just in time.

'In you come. In you come, the bell has rung. Do not delay. Your work is set, so together, let's start the day' called out Miss Lawford, whilst counting everyone back into the building.

The children began to trickle back into class, one by one. Their hearts were filled with the thrilling details and possibilities of what they had just heard. However, they each had the same one question on their minds; 'I wonder which side of the book my name is on?'

Back outside, Dexter began to question Terry.

'Hey, why did you lie yesterday?'

'When did I lie? I didn't lie!' Terry defended himself against such an accusation.

'My mother offered you a lift home, but you said your brother was picking you up.'

'Yeah, and he did.' Terry declared.

'But I saw you walk off past the school gates.' Dexter confessed.

'Do you work with the 'walking home police' or something?' Terry lashed back as he realized that he had been caught out in his lie.

'Where was your brother yesterday? Didn't he worry when he couldn't find you at the school gates?' Dexter innocently enquired.

'My brother has never picked me up at the school gates. I always meet him halfway, near the burger bar on the High Street.' Dexter stayed silent and looked on as Terry murmured, 'it was only a small lie. Your mum didn't find out, did she?'

'No, she didn't.' Dexter reassured him. Terry kept his head down and continued to mumble under his breath.

'It won't make a difference now, so why does it matter? A small lie is still a lie and I've been telling them for most of the year.' He kicked at the thin layer of snow in the playground and watched it puff up around him like a cloud of dust. 'I doubt I'm in the *'deserving'* side of the book anyway, so it makes no difference.' Terry shrugged his shoulders at Dexter.

'Well, you'll have to wait till Christmas Day to find out.' Dexter stated. A knowing smile crept across Terry's face as he looked Dexter in the eye.

'Maybe I won't have to wait that long.' Terry remarked. He swung his bag off his shoulder, opened it up and showed Dexter what it held.

The Book of Names sat tucked inside the contents of his scruffy bag. Dexter instantly gasped as his breath seemed to be snatched away from within him.

'Always the same two faces and always the last two to come in when the bell rings,' sang out Miss Lawford. 'Let me see you come in last again this week and seeing as you like it out here so much, you two will spend the entire week cleaning the playground.' She challenged the latecomers as they ran past her, into the school.

– CHAPTER NINE –

'so basically, you stole The Book of Names'

Dexter had to wait until lunchtime before he could trap Terry in a corner of the dining hall. He plonked himself down opposite him and demanded answers. Terry had scoffed down his lunch and had started on his dessert.

'What was that in your bag? Is it what I think it is?' Dexter demanded an answer.

'It's exactly what you think it is.' Terry leaned across and replied with his mouth full and an impish glimmer in his eyes. The moment had suddenly become very risky, so Dexter got up and made his way around the table to sit beside Terry.

'How did you get hold of it?' Dexter asked discreetly through his clenched teeth.

'Easy. As the dry-cleaner man was loading his van, I made a dash for it.' Terry explained.

'So basically, you stole *The Book of Names*.' Dexter concluded. The two boys spoke without looking at each other, which made them seem even more suspicious to the crowd around them. 'You really need to return it, Terry. This is not a good thing. You'll end up on the flip-reversed for a very long time.' Dexter's tone had a pleading quality which Terry clearly chose to ignore. He shoveled his rice pudding into his mouth and through his puffed-up cheeks, managed to speak.

'Well, I'm off home to check the names in the book.'

'You can't just walk out of the school.' Dexter's face contorted at the suggestion.

'Just watch me,' Terry spluttered as his face bulged across his cheeks. He walked over to the canteen staff and announced, 'Sir, I don't feel too well.' Terry bent over double and spewed out his mouth bursting load of pudding over Mr. Collins' shoes. He instinctively jumped back to avoid the onslaught of mess splashing over him. Unfortunately, he ended up slipping over and falling, thwack onto his backside and into the discarded rice pudding. A roar of disgusted 'eewwws' and 'yhaaak' echoed throughout the dining hall as the rest of the older children uncontrollably clapped and cheered along.

'Errrrm, sorry Sir, I told you I wasn't feeling too well,' Terry continued with his act whilst the rest of his pudding slowly dripped from his mouth. 'What shall I do?' he whimpered.

'Don't move! No! Don't speak, I'll get you to the nurse,' Mr. Collins assured the 'sick boy,' 'well, as soon as I can get up out of this… sludge.'

The odd chuckle could still be heard in class later that afternoon. Some of the children couldn't help but re-enact to each other what they had witnessed in the dining hall earlier. Hidden sniggers crept across the class and Miss Lawford was quick to quash the atmosphere.

'Stand up anyone, if you think it's funny when your classmate is unwell!' she demanded. A sudden silence swallowed up the noise and it now filled the room.

'Hey, look down there.' Lukas pointed out of the window to the front gate as he broke the quietness in the class.

'It's Terry with his older brother, Connor. He must have come to take Terry home.' Billy confirmed. Dexter sat in silence staring down at the front gate. He knew Terry's plan had worked to perfection and he would soon be at home alone with *The Book of Names*.

– CHAPTER TEN –

'if you're in it, you'll be under the 'T' letter'

Later that afternoon, Terry made his way up to his bedroom without a fuss. He spoke quietly as his act continued.

'I'm going to have a lie down until mum gets home. I already feel a little bit better anyway,' he informed Connor.

'I'll make you a sandwich and bring it up to you,' Connor replied, but Terry did not want to be disturbed by his older brother.

'It's okay, I'll have it when I come back down,' he said before he skulked upstairs, clutching tightly onto his rucksack. Terry shut the bedroom door and slumped to the floor and sat against it. He was heavy enough to slow anyone from coming into the room without warning and seeing that he shared the same bedroom with Connor, it was quite often the case. Terry shoved his arm deep into his rucksack and rummaged inside until he had a tight grip, then slowly pulled out *The Book of Names.*

'There you are... you little beauty,' he mumbled as his eyes fell upon it. Terry discarded the rucksack as he cradled *The Book* in both hands. He breathed in the moment as he felt the air around him brimming with an unknown excitement. *The Book* sat on his lap as he supported it in the palm of one hand. He peeled back the tissue papers that protected it. This was a tense moment for Terry. His heart made him believe that there may be the slightest of chances that his name was in *The Book*. However, his mind kept jarring with another thought; his head was telling him that he was very likely to be on the flip-reversed.

He delicately pinched the corner ends of the tissue paper and gently unraveled the wrapping that enveloped *The Book* until it was fully revealed. It was possibly the most vibrant colour red he had ever seen. It managed to steal Terry's breath for a split second, and he gasped before whispering to himself, 'Okay, here we go.' He opened the cover page. Terry's eyes scanned through the inviting pages of the book. Every line contained a different name and each one of them had been handwritten. The first page contained what looked like over a hundred names and Terry realised this was a task which was going to take much longer than he had planned.

He was only two pages through when he suddenly felt a quick nudge from the other side of the door jar into his back.

'Hey, what's going on in there?' Connor shouted from outside as he tried to open the door. 'What are you up to? You'd best not be touching my stuff in there!' His tone threatened whilst his stiffened finger prodded into the door.

'I'm not. I'm just reading… it's a new book from school,' Terry replied.

'Reading? It sounds as though you're getting worse. I'll tell mum to call a doctor when she gets in later.' Connor's sarcastic tone did not go amiss.

'Very funny,' Terry responded.

'Anyways, your friend is here to see how you're feeling.' Connor's voice faded as he walked off and plodded back downstairs.

'What friend? Who? Terry jumped to his feet and opened the bedroom door to find Dexter standing there holding an oversized card.

'Hi,' he said.

'What's that?' Terry enquired as he pointed at the card.

'It's a get-well card, for you. I made a big one because I was going to fill it with everyone's name and messages from our class this afternoon but… no one else wanted to sign it for you. Sorry.' Dexter apologetically revealed the inside of the card to show it off to Terry. 'Oh yeah, look, I'll show you this first! Miss Lawford was the first to sign it… and she put a kiss near her name, just there.' Dexter pointed at the precise location of the kiss. 'And I signed it on this side with a message as well, but no kiss.' Terry stared at the card intensely and couldn't stop his lips from curling with anger.

'I don't care about cards. I hate cards. Just as well, as I've never had one anyway.' Terry's gaze was broken by something more demanding and he re-focused his thoughts. 'Quick, get in here.' Terry yanked Dexter into his room and shut the door tight before he slumped up against it again. He pointed at his bed and spoke quickly. 'Anyway, thanks for the card. Throw it on the bed and come and sit down against the door.' Terry reached behind the door where he had hidden *The Book*. 'Sit down and look at this. I've opened it up and it's completely full of names.' Dexter tossed the card away and dumped himself against the door. His eyes instantly fixated on *The Book*. Terry flicked through the pages quickly as he showed a glimpse of the names contained on each sheet.

'How am I supposed to find my name in here?' Terry huffed, as he gestured his dilemma to Dexter.

'Well, you'll have to just read through the names.' Dexter made it sound very simple.

'That'll take me up until next Christmas to read all this,' said Terry, becoming agitated.

'Let me look for you,' Dexter said as he took hold of *The Book* and opened it up slowly. He turned over several pages and looked up at Terry. 'You're lucky, it's in alphabetical order,' Dexter said.

'And that makes me lucky, exactly how?' Terry asked.

'Well, it's in alphabetical order. It means all the letters are…' Terry's brow furrowed in frustration and Dexter was quick to spot his mood worsen and so explained simply. 'It means we can find your name quickly and won't have to waste time looking through it all.'

'Show me how,' Terry demanded. 'Please', he added.

'Let me see.' Dexter thumbed through the pages quickly and slowed down to a brief pause at the 'D' section. The moment seemed to cause a glint to reflect in his eye, which did not go amiss under the intense glare Terry had placed upon him.

'What it is?' Terry crashed in.

'I'm… oh, it's nothing, I'm just looking for something,' Dexter flustered back. He stopped at the section where the 'T' names began and presented *The Book* to Terry.

'If you're in it, you'll be under the 'T' letter,' Dexter instructed.

'What does that mean? Terry questioned. 'If I'm in it? Before Dexter had the chance to answer back, the bedroom door thudded open, pushing Terry over onto his knees as Connor poked his head around the door.

'Hey, gruesome twosome. What are you up to?' he asked.

'Nothing, we're just reading,' Terry responded as he shut *The Book*. 'We've finished now anyway.'

'Good, because your mum is here to pick you up,' Connor informed Dexter before leaving the room as quickly as he had entered.

'Okay, I'm off. See you tomorrow.' Dexter bounded up to his feet ready to go, only to turn and briefly pop his head back into the room again. 'Oh anyway, good luck.' He left, and Terry listened out for the thump of his footsteps as he ran down the stairs and left with a slam of the front door.

'Finally, I can get to work,' he whispered to himself. Terry opened *The Book* at 'T' and began his search.

– CHAPTER ELEVEN –

'watch out for the dream demons'

Two hours had passed by and, even after double checking, Terry had not found his name. He had hidden *The Book* under his mattress and was now sitting downstairs playing with his food.

'You've hardly touched that. Are you still feeling unwell?' his mother, Sandra asked as she made her way to the kitchen. 'I'll get you a lovely cup of tea, it will make you feel better.'

'What's the matter with you?' Connor chipped in. 'You'll never guess what I caught him doing this afternoon, mum,' he continued. Terry's tummy suddenly filled with a frantic fear that felt as if he had swallowed a bag of nervous butterflies.

'Whatever he says, no I wasn't.' Terry jumped to defend himself as Sandra returned with his favourite mug filled with freshly brewed tea.

'So, what wasn't he doing?' she asked.

'Don't believe a word he says Mum,' Terry pleaded.

'He told me he was… reading!' Connor started to laugh at the idea. 'I didn't realise he was sooo unwell,' he continued before taking hold of Terry by the scruff of his neck and playfully ruffling up his hair.

'Stop teasing your brother Connor and leave him alone,' Sandra ordered over her shoulder as she made her way back into the kitchen and returned with a tray. She sat down and began to feed her baby twins.

'Stop scrubbing my head so hard Connor, it hurts,' Terry implored.

'Oi, who's hurting who?' A heavy voice entered the room as Ray, the oldest brother walked in from work and plonked himself down on the sofa. Connor immediately let go of Terry and the two boys pushed each other apart.

'Terry was sick at school today. He spewed up all over the place and I had to go in and pick him up.' Connor updated Ray.

'Don't sit next to me if you're not feeling better,' Ray warned Terry.

'It's worse than that! I caught him reading twice this afternoon.' Connor relentlessly continued with his teasing.

'Oh no!' Ray shouted. 'He has got worse. Mum let's call for a doctor!' Ray and Connor fell about the front room belly laughing together.

'Stop teasing him, you two,' Sandra called out. The baby sisters began to giggle at all the commotion which seemed to amuse them endlessly. Terry stormed to the foot of the stairs and responded to his brothers.

'Leave me alone. I'm reading about Christmas!' As he stormed upstairs, the twisting echo of the boys' laughter chased Terry all the way up until it was shut out by the slam of the bedroom door.

'Right this is it!' Terry announced to himself with a desperate determination. He opened *The Book* at the start of 'T' again and for a third time, ran his finger through the list as he searched for his name. A short while later, Terry turned the final 'T' page and as he looked down the list, his eyes uncontrollably filled with tears. His worst fears had come true. He was not in *The Book of Names*.

'Why?' he whimpered to himself. His young eyes had now flooded, and salty tears began to stream down his face. Each tear was followed by another and another until they trickled down his cheeks and off his chin landing on the open pages of *The Book* in huge splashes of sorrow. 'Why is my name missing?' he blubbered. It was a question that led to another thought and Terry flustered through the pages to the 'D' section. His finger swiped through the names which were blurred through the tears in his eyes until it stopped on the name, Dexter James. A short paragraph followed the name. It read, *Log of Goods; helping his sister, keeping bedroom clean and tidy, being kind to others, etc.* Terry sniffed up his runny nose as he stared at Dexter's name before flicking through the pages and checking through the 'B' section. His finger fell on the name Billy Thomas. *Log of Goods; caring for his grandparents, helping his mother, being kind to others, etc.* Once again Terry flicked through the pages as another name popped into his thoughts and there it was, Ivy Richards, *Log of Goods; being kind to others, sharing time, helping her parents.* Every name he could think of appeared in the book, and it was followed on by their *Log of Goods*. 'Right then, this is it.' Terry murmured under his breath as he wiped his face dry with the cuffs of his shirt and sniffed hard again. He picked up *The Book* then flipped and reversed it onto its other side. The vibrancy of the blooming colour seemed to be dulled and had unexpectedly lost its sheen. Terry became anxious at the thought of his next move and twiddled on his fingers whilst attempting to calm himself. He gripped hold of *The Book* with both hands and muttered again. 'This is where it gets serious.' Terry opened the cover and picked open the first page. The number of names in this section was much less and they were typed at random. 'This shouldn't take as long,' he thought. The flip-reversed only contained a few pages of names. Terry locked his stare on the first page and began to scan through as he read down the list carefully from page to page. His breathing began to quicken and so did his heartbeat as he neared the end of the named list. Terry turned over to the last page and there it was. WHACK! Right out of nowhere. It felt like a sudden one-hundred-ton-train had come hurtling out of the pages and crashed into him, right between the eyes. There, in real print, he read his name, Terry Ruddock. *Flip-Reversed Log; uncaring, selfish and dishonest etc.*

Terry's glare was fixated on the log that followed his name and it took a moment for it to settle with him. He realised that the log was true; he couldn't remember the last time he helped or felt caring or shared anything. A wave of shame swept over Terry and he uncontrollably ripped out the pages and shredded them into small pieces with his bare hands. His heartbeat began to increase, and it pumped with a rage that he had never felt before. Terry turned *The Book* back to the original side and paused to stare at the title, *The Book of Names*. 'If I don't get a visit, then no one gets a visit,' he said to *The Book* and dived in amongst the pages as he pulled out each sheet one by one and ripped them each into more than ten pieces. He only managed to stop himself when the front and back cover remained in his hands and he was covered in torn scraps. Terry stood and kicked at the mess around him and the discarded pieces floated up and fell back down like snowflakes. 'I hate this. I hate all of this,' he raged. His anger burned until he felt himself tire, slow down and eventually come to his senses. Terry stood in the middle of his bedroom and it looked as though he had been caught in the middle of a snowstorm. He observed the mess around him and had no idea how he could ever explain his way out of it.

'Are you feeling okay up there?' Ray called up, checking on Terry.

'Errrrm, yes. I'm much better now.' Terry replied. It was enough to help him conjure up another dishonest plan and he bounded downstairs into the kitchen. 'Hi Mum!' he called out and waved as he passed the family who were still in the front room. He rifled through the cupboards and found exactly what he was looking for. He grabbed a black bin bag and quickly shoved it under his top and headed straight back up to his room. 'Bye Mum! Terry called out and waved again as he shot back up the stairs. Once inside his room he set about quickly collecting all the confetti-like evidence that he had furiously strewn around in tiny bits and pieces. A short while later, just as he took his last frantic grab of cuttings, the bedroom door swung open and Ray walked in.

'How are you feeling little man?' he enquired. That was enough of a cue for Terry and he did not hesitate; he shoved his last handful of scraps into the bag and quickly followed it by burying his face into the open end. He began coughing and spluttering and pretended to be sick all over again. He thrust the bag towards Ray who winced away from his brother's outstretched arm. 'Errrrgh! You must be joking!' Ray's voice echoed upstairs on the landing before he headed off downstairs to report what he had just seen. Terry gave it a few seconds before he followed his brother along with the bin bag tightly scrunched closed. Sandra was cradling the twins when she heard the commotion of what had just happened upstairs. Terry walked in trying to hand the bag over to either of his brothers who both reeled away in disgust.

'Connor take that and throw it in the bins please,' Sandra instructed.

'Errrrgh, no way am I touching that bag,' Connor objected.

'I haven't got time for this Connor, so please do what I say!' Sandra's voice rose and by her tone, Connor quickly realised her temper was close to breaking point. He reluctantly approached Terry and took the bin bag off him.

'You little runt! Connor jibed at his brother. However, Terry had learnt to always give as good as he got from his older brothers and pretended that he was close to being sick again but this time, Connor would be his target. 'Just you dare!' Connor said before leaving the house with his outstretched arm to the outside bins. The winter's night felt as though the cold had bitten him on his fingertips and so he tossed the bag in the general direction of the other bins and ran back in quickly. 'Oh! It's freezing out there.'

'Goodnight Mum, I'm going to bed.' Terry kissed Sandra and his twin sisters and made his way to bed.

'Goodnight love.' She said and watched him walk upstairs. 'Are you feeling better?' Sandra asked after Terry.

'Yes, much better now, goodnight.'

'Watch out for the dream demons,' Both Ray and Connor echoed.

'Shut up!' Terry yelled down over his shoulder and disappeared into his bedroom. He picked up his card and read his get well wish from his only friend.

'Hope to see you soon in class. Get well quick, from Dexter.' The kind and generous words were the last things he read that night before drifting off to sleep. A pang of guilt lay beside him for the rest of the night.

– CHAPTER TWELVE –

meanwhile, through the bitter cold night

Meanwhile, through the bitter cold of the evening, the night was slowly coming alive as hideous screeches pierced the silence of the night and young fox cubs called out to their mothers. The vixens were out scavenging the streets for food. They were wise and had become accustomed to the fact that dustbins were often loaded with valuable scraps of food. More enticing was the sight of a discarded bin bag which was easy to rip apart. The presence of this outside Terry's home was too inviting to let miss and the hungry foxes set upon it without pity. The moonlight glinted off their razor-sharp teeth as it took mere seconds for them to rip the bag into shredded pieces of plastic and spill its contents over the street before leaving, still hungry.

It wasn't long after the foxes had moved on that the next set of visitors started to come alive and prowl the area. Small tufts of curled fur darted through the lamplit street as squirrels danced around looking to pick up anything they could stash away. Pieces of fruit, leftover sandwiches, nuts, biscuits and especially for this time of year, even chocolate.

However, at this very moment in time, the street was filled with delicate pieces of paper from *The Book of Names*, all being lavishly blown around by the winter wind. It was very early in the morning and had anyone been up so late or awoken so soon and looked out of their window, they would have witnessed a most fantastic scene. Not only would the sight of something resembling a snowstorm billowing out of a bin bag seem unimaginable but seeing more than a hundred squirrels collecting scraps of torn paper and running along the street would have seemed more like a dream, rather than reality.

– CHAPTER THIRTEEN –

'what's going on in our local park?'

The next morning at school, Miss Lawford checked on Terry and then made sure he stood in front of the class and thanked Dexter for the card and his kind get well wishes.

'Dexter, thank you for your message and my card yesterday. I think it's the reason I am feeling much better today.' Terry announced. 'Thank you.' As he made his way back to his seat, the door swung open and Miss Wells, the head teacher popped her head in.

'A word please, Miss Lawford,' she said.

'Of course,' followed the reply and she swiftly made her way out into the corridor. Through the window in the door, Dexter could see that the two of them seemed to be deep in conversation and so he took the chance to speak with Terry.

'Well?' Dexter asked.

'Well, what? Terry replied, fully understanding the question.

'Don't waste time.' Dexter glanced back at the door. 'What happened? Did you find your name yesterday? he asked with caution.

'Yes,' it was a short but sharp reply from Terry.

'Excellent!' he thumped his fist down onto the desk in relief.

'Not really,' Terry's comment hit with a heavier thud. 'My name was on the flip-reversed.'

'What?' Dexter's squeal caused the entire class to turn towards the boys, but the children quickly redirected their attention back to the door as Miss Lawford came back into the room.

'Thank you, Miss Wells, I'll get the class ready.'

'Thank you. Let's gather at the school gates, in let's say ten minutes.' Miss Wells instructed before leaving for the next class along the corridor.

'Okay. We have ten minutes to prepare.' Miss Lawford announced to the class.

'Oh yes!' Ivy clenched her fist. 'Are we going out Miss? Please say yes,' she continued.

'Right, now we have nine minutes. If we are not downstairs in time, then we are going nowhere. Anyone else impatient enough to interrupt me and delay us with another question?' Miss Lawford asked the class. Her question was followed by several echoes of the sound 'sssshhhh,' which came from different corners of the room, all directed at Ivy.

'No Miss, sorry Miss,' Ivy mumbled under her breath. Miss Lawford continued.

'I've been informed that our local park, Peckham Rye Common has become a hive of activity this morning. There are journalists, radio reporters, television cameras and reporters who are interviewing locals at the site as we speak.'

'Oh, that is so cool.' Billy expressed his thoughts.

'So, by my count, we're now, down to six minutes.' Miss Lawford paused.

'As I was about to say, seeing that Peckham Rye Common is our local park and you are local residents, it has been decided that our school should attend in order to represent the area. So, without another moment's delay, please get yourselves quickly and quietly wrapped up warm and let's go and find out what's going on in our park.' Miss Lawford managed to generate a buzzing level of excitement amongst the children that was now close to exploding.

– CHAPTER FOURTEEN –

'we are all part of a real-life fairy tale'

The class stayed in line and traced Miss Lawford's footsteps along the pavement like ducklings following their mother, over the crossing and into Peckham Rye Park. As they neared the site, the clearer it became as to what was stirring the circus style atmosphere into a frenzy. The open expanse of green common they knew so well had truly changed overnight. It was now covered in a full forest which held a delicate rainbow haze that floated like fog through the mass of treetops. The teachers and children and everyone who approached the forest all did so with stolen gasps of astonishment. It was true, Peckham Rye Park had become a hive of activity and the children listened on to various radio interviews as they happened.

'It's so odd. My children were playing here only a few days ago. Now look at it!' said one bewildered parent to the reporter.

'It's the middle of winter, it's the middle of Peckham Rye Park, and over one night, a forest grows out of nowhere?' Another voice laughed in disbelief as they commented.

'Never mind all that! Look at this colourful mist floating past. It's so magical.' A third parent joined the conversation.

'And so, it seems, today, we're all part of a real-life fairy tale.' The reporter concluded her interview.

'The fairy tale of Peckham Rye Park!' They all sang together into the reporter's microphone and laughed out loud, as the frenzy continued to build. The children found themselves next to another interview about to start, but this one was for the television. They were rudely pushed aside by a heavyset cameraman and then shoved away by an equally brash television presenter as she was preparing to get her story.

'So, what did you actually see last night?' the reporter asked a man standing nearby.

'Well, as I was walking home, I was overtaken by hundreds of squirrels that ran past me into the park. They were carrying little clumps of paper and I watched them burying the pieces into the earth along with any other scraps they had picked up.' The man explained his version of events. 'Oh, and I found this blowing around last night.' The man stuck his fingers into his top pocket and pulled out something for the interviewer. 'I think it's one of the pieces that the squirrels were burying,' he said. To the entire class and the reporter, the scrap of paper looked exactly like what it was, a small scrap of paper. The interview quickly became boring for the class and a welcomed distraction came in the form of Lukas making a discovery not seen by anybody else.

'Hey! You guys. Come quick and have a look at this.' The group of children dispersed from the news reporter and made their way over to Lukas.

'Stay close together Class!' Miss Lawford called out as the children headed after Lukas, who was by now, standing at the base of a tree staring intently at the mystical fog that passed through its branches.

'What is it?' Dexter asked.

'Look at these trees,' Lukas insisted.

'Yes, we know they've all suddenly sprouted on the common. It's why we're here today,' Billy pointed out.

'No, look at them, really look,' Lukas said and pointed to the closest tree to them. The mystical feel of the haze glistened, with small bursts of random light. 'Oh, did you see it?' Lukas asked around. Then another starburst popped and then another and then followed by another. 'What about that time – did you see it?' The children looked on confused and shook their heads in response. 'That's impossible. Look, stand here.' Lukas moved aside and he gently guided Dexter into his position. 'Now look,' Lukas whispered into Dexter's ear. It only took a second before Dexter blinked his unbelieving eyes tight and tried to refocus again on the tree. Pop! Pop! Pop-Pop! The drifting starbursts of light shimmered again.

'Do you see it?' Lukas asked patiently. Dexter nodded. The boys looked at each other in amazement. 'Let's check the others,' Lukas demanded.

'What did you see?' Ivy stepped in between demanding to know.

'Your name!' Both boys said together. Dexter repositioned Ivy close to where he had stood and pointed at the tree. Sure enough, Ivy witnessed small bursts of light popping at irregular intervals. The light spectacle grew stranger still and as each flare popped, it released a word, the first of which was her name; Ivy Richards, appeared and then faded away to nothing. It was quickly replaced by three small light eruptions repeatedly popping, each of which released the words; 'generous', 'loving' and 'sharing'. Surrounding class members circled Ivy and watched the flares come and go.

'Yes, I saw your name too,' Leon called out from the crowd, 'and look, the words are popping again,' he pointed at the bursts. They all watched the words reveal and fade away yet again, 'generous', 'loving' and 'sharing'.

'This must be your tree,' Lukas stated.

'I found one too!' Billy called out. On inspection, the beautiful tree had another name glowing out of the light pops. 'Who's is it? Lukas asked before being pushed aside by Ivy.

'I see it. Look it reads Dexter James,' she pointed out before directing her attention to the next three flashes of light. 'There's more, look at the words. It says 'caring', 'honest' and 'loving'.

'That's your tree,' Lukas took great pride as he handed out the 'naming rights'. The children set off to search around the magical forest. Their excited voices seemed to fade out one by one and when Ivy caught up with them, they were all standing around a tree that looked very different amongst the other colourful trees in the forest. It was just a twisted old trunk of a tree with broken bark and gnarled branches growing in horrid jagged directions. There was no mystical haze floating through this tree and the flicker of light from each plop was horribly dull and muted to the colour of dirty snow.

'Can anyone see anything?' asked Lukas. Billy and Dexter traded places before both nodding a silent confirmation. Ivy cautiously approached the boys around the tree.

'What does it read?' she asked. The boys looked over at Terry and without hesitating, he nudged them aside and stepped in closer to their position. Terry cocked his head sideways as the name bubble flared and burst. He swallowed hard before speaking.

'It reads, Terry Ruddock,' he spoke softly.

'Oh.' Ivy for once was left, lost for words. The stunned silence around them was broken by the next three blops of dulled flashes for all to see. The words 'selfish' and 'uncaring' fell out and dropped around the tree. Before the two words could fade to nothing, a third word, 'dishonest' dropped like a stone.

A deafening hush swallowed up the children and they made their way back in silence, until they found more mist filled trees and light bursts for Lukas, Billy and the others from their class.

– CHAPTER FIFTEEN –

'you can't run away from the truth'

Back at school, the day was filled with nothing but talk of the colourful forest that filled the local park. However, Dexter had something else that needed discussing with Terry but had to wait until they were alone in the playground together.

'Look, Terry, I've had an idea. It's only been one day. Let's go back and give the dry-cleaner man a thank you card for the interview. I can design it tonight and we'll hand it to him tomorrow,' Dexter suggested.

'And what's the point of that?' Terry scoffed.

'Well, it's an easy plan. I'll distract him and that's when you can put *The Book* back under the counter.'

'Why would I do that?' Terry shrugged back.

'Because it's only been missing for two days. Maybe he hasn't even noticed yet. And if he has, when he finds it, he'll think he just misplaced it.' Dexter swelled with pride at the simplicity of his plan. 'See, I told you it was simple.'

'But it's not that simple really,' Terry announced.

'Why would you say that? We'll just go and put *The Book* back,' an unsure giggle escaped from Dexter's mouth. 'That's all we have to do.

It will be quicker than the time we spent interviewing him in the first place.' Dexter's brow was heavy as he spoke.

'It's not that simple because there is no *Book* to return,' revealed Terry. His words made Dexter feel as though he'd just swallowed a cannonball.

'What?' Dexter managed to cough up his question.

'I already told you, I found my name on the flip-reversed! Why, would I keep such a thing?' Terry snarled at Dexter.

'So, what did you do with it?' Dexter begged for an answer.

'I got rid of it. Okay? I ripped and ripped and ripped it to bits.' Terry fumed. 'Then I dumped the pieces outside for the bin men to take away. Alright? Finished. I got rid. There is no *Book*.' The confession had left Terry breathless and gasping for air.

'Have the bin men collected the rubbish yet? Dexter's voice was weak with exasperation.

'Why? What are you going to do? Stick all the pages back together?' Terry laughed at his own suggestion. 'You're too late and now, no one can find me on the flip-reversed.' Dexter stepped up to Terry and faced him nose-to-nose before he spoke.

'But you'll always be on the flip-reversed if you don't change the way you are.'

'Shut up!' Terry fumed and nudged Dexter in the face. 'You would have done the same if it was you on the flip-reversed,' stated Terry. Nobody had ever dared to get so close to 'The Terror' before and it caught him off guard. Terry pushed out hard. He shoved Dexter backwards causing him to tumble onto his backside with a thud. It wasn't clear if it was the push or the shove which caused Dexter's nose to bleed however, it did not go unnoticed by the others in the playground. Soon the two boys faced each other as a small crowd gathered around them.

'What about all the *'deserved'* names in *The Book?* Those names were just as important as yours,' said Dexter as he wiped away the blood that had dribbled into his mouth. 'But you put yourself ahead of hundreds of names. If you were deserving, then your name would have been on that side of *The Book*. together Terry stepped closer to Dexter and leaned down towards him.

'I'm off the flip-reversed and that's all that matters now.' Terry turned and looked at the standing crowd who slowly stepped aside, giving him enough space to walk away.

'That's all that matters!' Terry repeated to Dexter as he passed by him.

'Well, you can't run away from the truth; everything it said on your tree was true.' Terry stopped to listen to what Dexter had to say. 'You're selfish, uncaring, dishonest and probably, even worse. Who would ever want to be friends with someone like that? Now you know exactly why no one wanted to sign your card. You will end up alone.' Dexter had his last word. The crowd around him broke up and went off on their separate ways as Terry stormed off. Ivy approached Dexter and handed him a tissue as she helped him up to his feet.

'What was all that about? What were you two even talking about?' she asked.

'I wouldn't even know where to begin to try and explain to you,' he responded as he pressed the tissue against his bloody nose.

– CHAPTER SIXTEEN –

'stop disappearing… please stop fading away'

Later that evening, Connor called up to Terry who had spent most of the afternoon locked in his bedroom since coming home from school. Terry had been struggling with his feelings of guilt for hurting his only friend at school.

'Hey! Misery face! Come down and see this. Your school is on the television.'

'Stop lying! You're not going to catch me out!' Terry yelled back.

'Fair enough! I've just seen Miss Lawford as well. So, what's all this about a forest in Peckham Rye?' Connor yelled back upstairs at Terry. The words had an immediate effect and the urgent thud of Terry's footsteps pounding down the stairs ended with him jumping down the last three in haste. He burst into the lounge where Connor was sprawled across the sofa watching the television. Terry managed to catch the same interview halfway through that he had seen earlier that day.

'I was overtaken by hundreds of squirrels that ran past me into the park. They were carrying little clumps of paper and I watched them burying the pieces into the earth.' Terry listened intently to the interview and the man finished off by pulling a small piece of paper from his pocket and showed it to the interviewer. 'This is one of those scraps,' the man announced. Terry stepped nearer to the television and he focused on the close-up shot that the camera had zoomed in on. To his horror, it became very clear that the word said *'uncaring'*. Terry recognized the scrap paper and he knew it was a piece which he had ripped from the pages of *The Book of Names*.

'What did you do last night with that rubbish bag mum told you to throw away?' Terry asked his brother.

'Errrrm exactly what she asked me to do; I threw it away,' said Connor.

'Yes, but where did you throw it exactly?' Terry pushed on carefully.

'I tossed it over the bins. What's the big deal?' Connor became impatient. 'Anyway, forget about it. The bin men have taken it by now.'

'Forget about it!' Terry squealed. 'The bin men haven't taken it because you didn't put it in the bin as mum asked you.' He continued just as Sandra walked into the lounge with the twins. 'The foxes or cats must have ripped up the bag and then the squirrels took everything else,' Terry blubbered.

'Connor, get up off that sofa and go and heat the milk for your sisters, please.' Sandra instructed before turning to Terry. 'What are you talking about Terry? Help me tidy up the toys in here.' Terry scrambled around on the floor, collected up the clutter and dropped it all into the nearby toy box before he spoke again.

'It's all Connor's fault there's a forest on Peckham Rye Park. The squirrels took all the bits of paper and buried them. Now each piece has grown into a tree which belongs to each child from *The Book of Names* and that's exactly why a forest has appeared overnight.' Terry stated.

'*The Book of* what are you talking about? Just, listen to yourself, Terry. How do you know who the trees belong too?' Sandra huffed; her voice full of exasperation. 'Terry, I don't think I have the energy for this today.' The sight of Connor returning from the kitchen with two bottles of warm milk for his twin sisters made them both squeal with excitement.

'He keeps talking about squirrels and stuff,' Connor tried to explain. 'I have no idea what he means but I think he's still unwell from yesterday,' he added.

'I'm going to my room because no one understands,' Terry announced. He headed off up to his room and slammed the door shut tight as he plonked himself onto his bed.

That evening, Terry reflected on his thoughts and how he never really meant to push Dexter onto the floor as it was Dexter who had shown him more friendship than anyone else. Terry picked up his 'oversized get well card' and kept reading the message again and again as he recalled Dexter's words that 'nobody else wanted to sign' it. Dexter's message comforted him, and Terry read it over repeatedly until his eyes became too heavy to keep open. He slowly blinked himself towards a deep sleep... when... he sat himself up and checked his card again. To his horror, he noticed that each of the kind words slowly started to disappear, one letter at a time. Terry had no idea what he could do to stop the letters fading away and so did the first thing that came to mind. He shut the card tight and whispered quietly.

'Stop disappearing... please stop fading away.' Terry slowly opened the card and peeked inside. The card was now as empty as it was when it was new, just before a single pen or pencil stroke had touched any part of it. Terry had seen the gentle and kind words fade away. He slammed the card shut again as he began to softly sob, his head buried in his hands. His attention was suddenly gripped by a hideous sound that started to slowly screech into his ears. It grew louder and sharper and it seemed as if each wall in his room was throwing the sound back directly at him. Its echo was so vicious, he was sure it would vibrate every tooth out of his mouth. Terry felt the noise scratch across his skin, causing the hairs on the back of his neck to stand on end as he tried to muffle out the sound by clasping his hands over his ears. A tremor caused the card to lift open and Terry realised the noise was coming from within it. He looked on as various letters began to scrawl themselves across the card. Each jagged letter carved itself to create words that fell in front of Terry's eye line. He saw each word grow. 'Selfish'. 'Uncaring'. 'Dishonest'. Terry slammed the card shut hard as he yelled, 'No!' The shock caused him to jump and his body jolted the card off the bed. A cold sweat had sent a shiver through his bones and Terry felt delirious.

With his arm extended and fingertips outstretched, he managed to flick open the card. Terry cautiously looked over the bed's edge at the card again and saw the message and get well wish from Dexter had returned. Terry felt confused up until his senses alerted him that he had abruptly awoken from a nightmare. Although the freakish dream felt so real, he had no intention of living it. He carefully placed the card beneath his bed out of sight, tucked himself under his covers and fell asleep again.

CHAPTER SEVENTEEN

'maybe it's much too late for this one to bloom'

The next morning, Terry came down for breakfast and joined his mother and twin sisters in the kitchen.

'What's for breakfast, Mum? I'm starving,' Terry announced as he sat down.

'Well I'm not surprised, you didn't come down for your tea last night,' Sandra said as she patiently spoon-fed the twins, filled the toaster with two slices of bread and put the kettle on to boil.

'But why didn't you call me?' Terry's voice quivered.

'Call you? I called out four times and yelled twice. Then, I came up with your tea, but you were tucked up sleeping tight. You looked so peaceful. I didn't want to disturb you.'

'But I missed having my tea last night and it was fish fingers, my most favourite,' Terry exhaled.

'So, thank your lucky stars that your day has started off so well this morning.' Sandra said as she placed down a warm mug of tea for Terry.

'What is going so well for me this morning?'

'You've got fish fingers on toast for breakfast.' Sandra smiled as she presented him with his breakfast. Terry's face cracked with a satisfying grin that spread across his face and he hid it by burying his face into his fresh mug of tea.

'Thanks, Mum, you're the best,' Terry mumbled, which in turn, earned him a precious kiss on the head from his busy mother. Just then, Ray came into the kitchen and poured himself a glass of milk. He downed it in one gulp, pausing only to speak to Terry before munching on a banana.

'Get your boots on little man, it's started snowing out there.'

'Oh, does that mean there's no school today?' Terry's voice was full of hope.

'No, it means finish your breakfast and get your boots on because we're going to be late for school. And I want to go and see that forest everyone is talking about.'

'What? Why do you want to see that? It's rubbish. I saw it the other day and it's just trees covered in coloured fog.' Terry tried to put Ray off from visiting the newly grown forest.

'Hurry up and get your boots on, I'm waiting outside for you.' The door closed behind him and Terry knew he was left with no choice. He grabbed his unfinished fish fingers and toast and stuffed it into his blazer pocket. He changed into his boots, kissed his mother and sisters and headed outside after his brother.

Terry hesitantly followed Ray through the park gates and approached the lush growth which had unexpectedly blossomed. The vibrant display had not only become a news story but also a local attraction for the residents as well as visitors from near and far. The new trees looked even more magical as a delicate snowfall had settled around them early in the morning.

'Hey Terry, come and look at this sorry looking tree,' Ray called out as he pointed to the lone rotted trunk that sat twisted and jagged amongst the others. 'I don't know why anybody hasn't cut this one down yet,' Ray continued. A passer-by who was walking his dog overheard Ray and responded.

'You're right! It spoils all the others too. Perhaps if I get a chance on my evening walk, I'll bring an axe and cut it down tonight. At least it will improve the view,' he said. Terry's heart pained at the careless comment from the man and he felt worse when the nearby dog ran at the ragged tree, raised its back leg up and sprinkled on it. Terry glanced over at Dexter's, Ivy's and Billy's trees. He could see the colourful star bursts revealing the same words over and over again as the day before.

'Well, maybe all the others started like this one and this is the last of them to change,' Terry responded. He tried to defend the gnarled tree and as he spoke, a small dulled burst, popped again revealing his name, 'Terry Ruddock'. It was closely followed by the plop of the same three words over again; 'selfish', 'uncaring' and 'dishonest' randomly repeated.

'It looks like it's much too late for this one to bloom like the others,' said Ray. It left Terry standing flabbergasted. It appeared that the two adults as well as the dog were completely oblivious to the light bursts that were popping around them. The revealing pops only seemed to be visible to children.

'It will be too late if it doesn't improve by this evening. Chop! Chop!' threatened the passer-by. His comment caused himself and Ray to laugh out loud together. Even the dog seemed to join in, not only barking excitedly but with its tail wagging so fast and hard, Terry was convinced it would take off like a helicopter.

'Ray, I'm going to school now, otherwise, I'll be late.' Terry's voice was full of exasperation. 'I'm okay to go alone from here,' he announced. Although the tree in the park was not as colourful as the others around it, Terry felt attached to it because it bared his name within the star bursts of light. A sudden sadness began to flood Terry's heart at the thought that his tree would be chopped down because it hadn't been given a chance to grow like the others. 'See you tonight, I'm going to school!' he called to Ray before setting out on his way.

– CHAPTER EIGHTEEN –

'he's a real-life hero'

Terry hadn't long set off before a frightened mewing sound coming from an unknown direction caught his attention. He plodded along the road until a woman holding a young child blocked his path. They both seemed to be in a state of panic whilst staring up into an Oak tree. Upon his approach, the mewing grew louder and more desperate, which in turn, caused her child to begin crying.

'Excuse me,' said the woman. 'I wonder if I could ask you to just watch my kitten,' she asked whilst pointing up into the nearby tree. 'The poor thing is still a little excitable and so she's climbed out of the window and made her way along the branches. It now seems that she's stuck up there.' Terry followed the woman's pointing finger into the tree and he spotted the playful kitten sitting on a branch.

'Oh yeah, I see her,' he confirmed.

'I just need to pop in and fetch my phone to call for help. Could you please keep your eye on her till I return?' she asked, whilst trying to keep a grip on the child who was by now twisting around on her shoulders, almost drowning in her own tears.

'Errrrm,' Terry hesitated, 'okay then, but I can only stay for one minute, I'm on my way to school.'

'Oh, thank you so much. I'll be just one quick minute,' she confirmed before running up into her house. Terry kept his sharp eye on the kitten who had curiously climbed beyond its capacity and was now resting on a branch, pawing at the nearby leaves. Terry felt quite comfortable that he had the whole situation under control until he spotted a dustbin truck pull up across the road. That one minute of calmness suddenly changed. The bin men jumped out and dragged the nearby bins towards the truck, which in turn lifted them up and emptied them into the back of the vehicle. It was an everyday activity that Terry had seen many times. However, to a kitten, Terry imagined that it looked like a giant hungry robot mouth being wheeled through the streets, being vigorously fed as it chomped through the contents of the dustbins. The noise of the truck vibrated along the street and up the trunk of the tree, which caused the kitten to slip and slash out a claw at anything within its reach. The kitten panicked, moving to the edge of its branch and slipped as the truck across the road guzzled everything that was shoved into its gaping mouth. The kitten managed to cling to the tree trunk by using its tiny extended claws, but there was not much hold in them for a baby feline.

'Oh no!' Terry shouted. He threw his rucksack onto the floor and stepped up onto the bonnet of a parked car. He walked onto its roof and used it as a stepping stone onto a van which was parked behind it. He took a quick look up at the kitten which was now only clinging to the tree with one paw and yelping for help. 'Hold on, little one!' He called out before jumping from the van up onto the tree. Terry shimmied himself along the tree. His weight was now too heavy for the branch he was on and so he delicately laid himself along the leafy stem which began to bow down, leaning him closer to his target. The kitten was still just out of his grasp and Terry needed to do some quick thinking in finding a way to get the kitten nearer to him. 'Hey little friend, maybe this will tempt you closer,' he said as he reached into his blazer pocket and pulled out a half-eaten fish finger. Terry extended his reach closer and offered his snack to the dangling kitten. 'Look what a delicious treat I have for you,' he mumbled. The tasty temptation did the trick and it encouraged the kitten to swing his other paw up and slowly pull itself a little further, just enough to allow Terry to lengthen his fully outstretched reach. The branch rocked just enough, and he managed to grab the kitten by the scruff of its neck and pull it to safety. Unfortunately, the tiniest extra weight of the kitten was too much for the branch and it curved at an angle that toppled Terry out of the tree. His reflexes were instant, and he took a tight grip on the nearest flexible stem, which miraculously, lowered him out of the tree. It placed him just behind the woman who, upon her return, had now become curious as to Terry's whereabouts. She was speaking on the phone whilst her child was still hysterically sobbing and now blowing tearful bubbles from its nose. The child now started yelling and pointing over her mother's shoulder at Terry and the cute bundle he held in his arm.

'Kitty! Kitty! Kitty!' The child's excitement caused the woman to turn and look at what the fuss was about.

'Hello,' Terry just smiled as he had no idea of what to say next.

'Oh, where did you come from?' The woman jumped as she turned around.

'Errrrm, from up there.' Terry pointed up into the tree. 'Here you are. She probably only has eight lives left by now.' He handed the kitten over to the woman whilst it was still guzzling down the fish finger. With the kitten in one arm and the child in her other, the woman awkwardly spoke on her phone.

'I'm sorry, there's no emergency now. A very kind boy has helped me. The kitten is out of the tree and safe from any harm,' she explained. The sight of the kitten in her mother's arms calmed the crying child instantly. 'Hey, what's your name?' the mother asked.

'I'm Terry.'

'His name is Terry,' the woman spoke back down the phone.

'Oh, Terry our hero!' She leaned over and kissed him on the top of his head. 'We both thank you very much,' she continued.

'That's alright, I have to go. I'll be late for school,' Terry blushed and faffed around as he turned and kicked his way through the morning snowfall to school.

'Yes, it was very nice of him and he's a real-life hero for helping,' Terry heard the woman say on the phone. The kind words filled him with a joy that he had never felt before and as he ran off, her voice faded out of earshot. The snow couldn't slow Terry down and the feeling he had seemed to propel him along the white dusted street.

– CHAPTER NINETEEN –

'you're an absolute credit to your mother'

As Terry neared his school, he stopped at a junction before carefully crossing the road. He noticed a car abruptly parking at the side of the road and its driver step out and begin to unload several bags of shopping.

'I'm not driving down this road. It looks too snowy. You'll have to walk it from here,' said the driver. Terry then caught sight of who the driver was talking to. It was an old woman struggling to step out from the back of the car. 'Anyway, it will cost you extra to drive through the snow,' the driver continued.

'But I don't have any extra money. Is it possible please to help me carry the bags across the road at least? I'm not too steady on my feet, not even with this walking stick,' the old woman pleaded politely.

'I'm afraid I can't help. Any extra means it costs more. You know with Christmas coming up and all that, the season of goodwill and whatever,' the driver replied.

'But I already paid you to take me home. I can't afford any extra.' The driver shook his head and shrugged his shoulders, indicating that he had no intention of helping the old lady carry her bags. It was also clear to Terry that the old woman was not able to carry the bags herself and so he approached her, asking if he could help.

'Excuse me, I'm just on my way to the school at the end of the road. If you like, I think I can spare a minute, so if we're quick I can help you carry them home,' he explained.

'I'd be careful if I was you, madam. Why would a rascal offer any help?' the driver spoke his thoughts aloud.

'You can drive away now, I'm not sure I care for your thoughts,' the old lady turned her back on the driver and spoke to Terry directly.

'Well, thank you, young man. That's a very generous gesture,' she said. They both watched the driver skid off along the road as he sped away.

'You hold my arm, and I'll take you across the road. Then, I'll pop back for your bags. It shouldn't take long.' Terry assured the old woman. She took hold of Terry's arm and they slowly walked across the road, step by step, leaving fresh footprints in the snow.

'This is so kind of you to help. I'm very nervous about falling over,' she explained as she crossed the road with Terry. 'I don't quite repair as fast as I used to, so I have to be very careful,' she explained as they walked with care.

'It's okay, I've got your arm. If you fall, it will be a soft landing as you'll probably land on me anyway,' Terry joked.

'I'm sorry, I don't know your name young man,' the old lady chuckled to herself. 'How can I tell my friends how wonderful you have been if I don't know who you are?' she continued as they crossed.

'My name is Terry, but most people call me Terror,' he shrugged.

'Terror? I find that very hard to believe,' she claimed. 'I'm very pleased to have met you, Terry. My name is Violet and as I'm a little older than you are, you can call me Mrs. Wilson.' As they reached halfway across the road, Mrs. Wilson began to take deeper breaths and started to walk at a pace that slowed down to just standing. 'Oh, I'm totally out of breath. I don't think I can take another step,' she panted.

'Well I can't just leave you halfway, I have to get you home without sliding and slipping all over the road.' Terry took a moment to think to himself. 'Oh, that's it! Mrs. Wilson, I'll need to borrow your walking stick please?'

'Oh no, you haven't hurt yourself, have you?' she asked full of concern.

'No, it's just that I have an idea.'

'Thank goodness for that.' Terry darted off over to the shopping bags, rearranged the contents and returned with an empty bag.

'Okay, Mrs. Wilson, I need you to trust me and step into this bag.'

'Of course, I trust you, you've got me halfway, haven't you? But stepping into a shopping bag?'

'Please trust me,' Terry assured her and held out his hand and helped Mrs. Wilson step into the shopping bag. 'Now, I need your walking stick, please.' He threaded the curved end of the walking stick through the bag's handles and he spoke in the poshest tone of voice he knew. 'Okay, your majesty, your carriage awaits.'

'Oh, this is very exciting,' Mrs. Wilson revealed.

'Are we ready, ma'am?' Terry asked before he gently pulled on the walking stick and it slowly tugged the bag onto the fresh snow which became super smooth. Mrs. Wilson glided over it with ease.

'I wasn't expecting this,' Mrs. Wilson yelped as she floated over the snow standing in her bag. A neighbour's curtain twitched as someone peeked out to see the excitement on the street. However, Mrs. Wilson wasted no time in waving like royalty at anyone interested in looking on.

Having delivered Mrs. Wilson to her front door in one piece, Terry offered a helping hand once again so that she could step out safely. He returned to the shopping bags on the other side of the road and started to line them up in a row. He threaded the walking stick through each of their handles and pulled the stick until its curved handle held the bags together.

'Okay, if I can't lift you bunch of bags, then I'll slide you along the snow too,' he whispered to the shopping. He then pulled on the stick and as he planned, they slid along the soft snow, following him across the road, along the path and right up to the front door. 'Special delivery!' Terry bellowed, his chest close to bursting with pride.

Mrs. Wilson's face was beaming. She realised she would have had no chance of getting herself or the bags to the house and through the snow alone.

'Let me tell you something, young man. You are an absolute genius. Wait right there, I have something for you.' She reached into one of the shopping bags and pulled out a box of mint chocolate cookies. 'These are my favourites and I'd like to share them with you as a thank you from me. And this is a little extra because it's Christmas and you made it so much fun.' She pushed a clean folded twenty-pound note into his small palm. Terry looked at the note whilst his eyes overflowed with a look of astonishment.

'But you said you didn't have any money. I didn't help you for money Mrs. Wilson, you don't have to pay me,' he whimpered.

'I wasn't going to give that horrible driver any more money,' she replied.

'I don't think my mum will be happy with me taking this money from you.' Terry handed back the money to Mrs. Wilson, but she clasped her hand around Terry's and pushed it back at him.

'Please tell your mother to come and see me if she has a problem and I'll tell her how charming you have been in helping me and how much fun it was, but most of all, what a credit you are to her.' Her eyes beamed a look of joy as she spoke.

'Thank you.' Terry pushed the money deep into his pocket for safe keeping. 'I have to go, I don't want to be really late,' he said and dashed off closing the front gate behind him, only to briefly return to the gate and call out, 'Merry Christmas to you, Mrs. Wilson!'

'Happy Christmas to you, Terry,' she called back and watched him run along to school.

– CHAPTER TWENTY –

'who wants to be friends with someone like you?'

Terry skidded around the corner and hurled himself through the gates. He realised he was already late as there was nobody left in the playground. He sped along the corridor and was temporarily stopped in his tracks by an unknown voice echoing off the walls as it bellowed out around him.

'Stop running and walk!' He immediately slowed down to a fast walking pace and as he turned out of sight, shot off continuing at speed until he reached his class door and came to a sudden halt. He grabbed at the door handle and almost twisted it off the door as he entered.

'Sorry, I'm la…' he started but was instantly met by silence. The room was empty, and Terry was left confused as to the whereabouts of the entire class. A gentle tap on his shoulder caused him to turn and he was met by Miss Goode.

'I imagine you're wondering where the rest of your class is. Am I correct?' she asked. Terry nodded back in silence.

'Well, all those who were here on time this morning, have gone on another visit to the Fairy Tale Forest,' Miss Goode explained, 'you were the only one who was late today.'

'Can I go and catch them up, please?' Terry asked preparing to speed off to the park.

'Of course, you can… NOT! Go and catch them up? You were late coming in and so you've missed your chance.' Terry felt all hope within him deflate.

'But I've had a really hectic morning Miss Goode and it wasn't my fault.'

'Oh, it's been a really hectic morning for you, has it?' The tone of her sympathetic voice was strangled by sarcasm as she listened to Terry's story. 'And to make it worse still, none of it was your fault, was it?' she continued. Terry shook his head and then changed to a quick nod and then to a shake again. 'You seem very confused, so let's spend some time in my office. First, you can write a letter of apology to your class for being late and making them wait for you. Then, if they still care at that point, you can explain to them why you were late.' Terry nodded.

Terry spent the next hour in silence together with Miss Goode in her office. He'd been told that she had 'tons of paperwork to get through,' so he spent the time with his head buried into his exercise book with nothing but the sound of his pencil scrawling frantically. The sound of the clock ticking against him could only be heard when he stopped writing. He was determined to finish his letter of apology to the class before they returned but it felt as though time had slowed down so much, he would have had the time to write an individual letter to each class member. Outside, it was still delicately snowing and even by now, it looked as though the snowflakes were falling in slow motion. Miss Goode noticed that the scrawling sound had stopped, and that Terry's attention was focused on the delicate flakes that fell past her window.

'Okay, seeing that it's not snowing so bad, go and get some fresh air for fifteen minutes. And then straight back up here, please. Your class will be back soon,' Miss Goode instructed Terry and he did not hesitate. He wrapped himself up with his coat and scarf and headed down to go outside. Terry strolled around kicking randomly at small snow tufts in the playground. It was a moment that left him feeling odd and left out. He had never felt such silence in a place that would normally be pulsating with the excited sound of children playing games and telling stories. He realised that he was very used to noises and sounds in his life. His home was full of them for a start. If it wasn't his older brothers always teasing him, it was his baby sisters either crying or playing loudly. Within the silence of the playground, Terry heard Dexter's words in the back of his mind as they echoed out: 'Who would ever want to be friends with someone like you? Not one person wanted to sign your card.' The words now seemed to fill the playground and all Terry could see in the snow were the words; 'selfish', 'uncaring' and 'dishonest'. The words chilled Terry more than the snow and he turned to go back in.

– CHAPTER TWENTY-ONE –

'I'm just Terry'

As Terry headed back, he caught the sight of a thin white-haired man wearing what looked like pyjamas. He was standing at the school gates staring back into the school. Terry cautiously walked towards the man. Although he kept more than an arm's-length away from the gate, Terry could see that not only was he wearing pyjamas, but he was also standing barefoot, his feet buried in the snow.

'Oh, hello?' Terry said. The man stared back with his eyes wide open. 'Are you okay?' Terry asked, which prompted the man to shake his head. 'Are you looking for someone?' Terry questioned.

'Yes.' He now nodded.

'Who are you looking for? Maybe I can help you find them.'

'I'm looking for me. This is my school,' the man said, and his words caused Terry to take a small step back.

'Aren't you cold? he asked and watched the man shake his head in response.

'It's just that you're standing in the snow with bare feet.' Terry pointed down.

'I'm cold now.' Terry was fully aware that some old people could feel the cold more than others due to his grandad's ill health. He took a moment to think and then slowly peeled off his scarf, stepped up to the gate and handed it through the rails.

'Here put this on.' The old man reached through the gate and as he took the scarf, Terry noticed just how cold the old man was as his whole arm was shivering.

'What's your name?' Terry asked but the old man looked blankly back at him and shook his head. 'I think you are like my grandad; he sometimes forgets things too. Errrrm, where do you live?' Terry tried another question only to be met with the same look of nothing. A feeling of panic started to hit Terry as he felt trapped with the situation, he found himself in. He wanted to run back into school and find Miss Goode, but he remembered that every time his grandad was left alone, he would walk off and get lost. Terry looked around the playground and noticed the tufts of snow he had kicked earlier.

'Oh yes, that's it!' He jumped with excitement. 'I'll take you home.' Terry cautiously walked out of the front gate and stood next to the old man. He clasped his stone-cold hand and felt his thin icicle-like fingers wrap around his small hand. Terry looked up at the old man and asked, 'Are you ready?' The old man nodded and muttered under his breath back at Terry as his grip on his hand tightened harder.

'Cccold. Vv… vvv… very cccold.' He struggled to speak.

'Please follow every single footprint, starting with this one.' Terry pointed to the snow-covered road ahead of them. 'Step into each foot as we walk,' he said and led the old man back into every crisp imprint that he had already left in the snow, tracing the original steps one-by-one back to his home. To Terry's relief, the footprints did not go too far, and they followed them until they turned into one of the houses a few doors along from Mrs. Wilson's home. Terry led the old man up to the front door and rang the bell. The door opened and the two of them were greeted by the old man's wife. She was clearly flustered yet ecstatic at the same time.

'Oh, where have you been, Jim? I've been worried sick about you.' She clung to the old man and squeezed him tight, pressing her head close into the hollow of his chest. 'I even telephoned the emergency services,' she said. 'Quickly, you need a hot bath, I can feel you're frozen to the bone.' She ushered the old man upstairs and turned to face Terry, 'My name's Francis and that is my husband, James Miller. I really can't thank you enough,' she whispered to him. 'He's started wondering off more often lately,' Francis continued before asking, 'what's your name young man?'

'I'm Terry. My friends call me... I'm just Terry,' he answered. 'Errrrm, Mr. Miller was just passing our school and I think the cold confused him, so he forgot where he lived.'

'He used to be the Headmaster at that school many years ago,' Francis said. 'How did you find out where we live?'

'The snow turned out to be lucky. I said let's follow the footprints back and so, here we are. My grandad wonders off as well sometimes,' Terry explained. Francis offered him a hot cup of tea to warm up. 'Thanks, but I really must go as I think I'm in a lot of trouble. I'm sure Miss Goode's breath will probably warm me up when she's telling me off.' Terry confessed before turning to leave.

– CONGRATULATIONS TO YOU! –

you have just completed your 100 pages plus

it's official – you are now a MeMBER

– CHAPTER TWENTY-TWO –

'please come out to the front of the class'

Terry ran back into school and headed straight up to Miss Goode's office, where she was still busy sorting out her paperwork. He burst in and headed straight to his desk.

'I'm so sorry I'm back late, Miss Goode,' he said before sitting down.

'Well, would you like to at least entertain me with an excuse for your lateness?' she sighed as she asked.

'I don't want to be dishonest with you, Miss Goode, but I'm not sure if a lie will be more believable than the truth.' Terry announced.

'Oh okay, so, you met Father Christmas and offered to help load the presents onto his sleigh, before feeding the reindeers.' Miss Goode reeled off her very unbelievable scenario which left Terry equally confused. 'Let's start with the truth, shall we?' she responded with a tone of intrigue.

'Well, the truth is I found an old man in pyjamas walking barefoot in the snow. It was Mr. Miller, he used to be the Headmaster here and he didn't know where he lived. I wanted to come and ask you for help, but I was scared he would walk off and get lost like my grandad always does. So, I took him home by following his footsteps backwards in the snow.

'This was all after I climbed into a tree this morning with a fish finger sandwich to rescue a kitten that was trapped high on its branches. And having done that, I helped Mrs. Wilson, who was afraid of breaking her bones in the snow. So, I had an idea to slide her across the road in a shopping bag with her own walking stick which worked a treat and she loved it. Oh, and then I hooked up her shopping and pulled that across for her too. She said she was so grateful so rewarded me with mint choc cookies, which I've never had before and a twenty-pound note, which I've never had or held before. And that's it. That's the truth.' Terry stopped to take a breath. He looked on and before Miss Goode could respond her door opened and Miss Lawford popped her head in.

'Hello Julia, I just wanted to let you know that we're back now.' She said before looking over at Terry and ordered him up and out. 'Come on, you. Get back into your class.'

Terry followed Miss Lawford down to his class and as he entered the room, he saw every single face in the class turn and look at him. 'Sit in your place please, Terry,' Miss Lawford instructed him. He quietly sat himself down at the table but there was an uncomfortable feeling that prickled Terry's skin every time he made eye contact with his classmates. Unknown to Terry, it was the heavy burden of guilt that he was still feeling as he came face to face with everyone whose name was written in *The Book*. The sudden realisation that he was responsible for throwing away the pages that contained the names of the *'deserved'* left him smothered in shame.

'Hey!' Ivy leaned over and whispered under her hand. 'Have you heard what's happened to your tree?'

'What! Has it happened already?' Terry's voice wobbled as he desperately tried to stop any tears from filling his eyes. 'It had nothing to do with that busybody dog walker,' he huffed.

'It's really different there now,' Lukas informed Terry.

'Yeah, everyone's talking about it,' Billy butted in.

'Whatever,' Terry responded with a broken heart.

'Hi, what's up?' Dexter leaned across and spoke to Terry.

'You wouldn't believe what kind of a morning I've had,' he replied.

'I'm sorry, I didn't mean it when I said you're like your tree,' Dexter whispered.

'I'm sorry, I…' Terry didn't get a chance to finish his apology. A knock at the door was followed by Miss Wells popping her head in and calling Miss Lawford outside into the corridor.

'A quick word please, Miss Lawford.'

'Yes, of course,' she replied. 'Class, I'd like you to start thinking about the Fairy Tale Forest and what you think about the unexpected change.' And on that instruction, Miss Lawford headed out into the corridor. As the door opened, a robotic sounding voice echoed outside, and it caught the attention of the children in the classroom.

'Did you hear that? There's a policeman outside, I heard his radio,' Billy announced.

'What are the police doing here?' Ivy enquired with a serious look in her eye.

'Someone has done something serious that they shouldn't have,' Billy answered.

'What have you done, Terry?' asked Lukas.

'Why do I always get the blame? What makes you think the police are here for me? Terry defended himself.

'Well, I only did it because I thought it would help,' Ivy confessed, but her table of friends had no idea what she was talking about and so chose to ignore her comment. The door swung open and the crowd in the corridor trickled into the classroom as a blanket of silence covered the entire room. Miss Lawford entered first, and she was followed by Miss Wells, who turned and spoke over her shoulder.

'This way please, Sergeant Jenkins.' A soft gasp darted between the children as the uniformed police Sergeant entered the room.

'I told you it was serious. Look, he has three stripes on his sleeves,' Billy took great pleasure confirming. The three adults headed to the front of the class and stood in silence. The children stared back in anticipation.

'Terry Ruddock, please come out to the front of the class,' Miss Wells ordered, and each of her words seemed to fall like a lead balloon.

The children around the table looked at Lukas, who sat back with a shrug and an expression of 'I told you so' plastered over his face. The silence in the class was only broken by Terry's chair as it scraped across the floor when he stood up and began his long walk to the front. His every step was followed by all eyes in the classroom, although to Terry, it felt as though every eyeball in the whole world was watching him. Miss Goode unexpectedly entered the class but was greeted with a heavy and serious atmosphere that filled the room.

'Oh, am I interrupting something? she asked from the door.

'No, no, please come on in,' said Miss Wells. 'In fact, could you call in the gentleman waiting in the corridor, please.'

'Yes of course,' Miss Goode replied and disappeared outside for a moment before returning with the man waiting in the corridor. To Terry's absolute horror, Miss Goode had returned with the man from the dry-clean shop who walked over and stood beside Police Sergeant Jenkins. Terry looked at Dexter who had already buried his face into his hands mumbling to himself under his breath and slowly shaking his head.

'Do you know this gentleman, Terry?' asked Miss Wells.

'He's the dry-cleaner man, I think,' Terry whispered.

'You think? You interviewed him just a few days ago.' Miss Wells was quick to respond.

'Oh yes, he's the dry-cleaner man.'

'Do you have any idea why he is here today?' she asked. Dexter looked up at Terry and he discreetly shrugged his shoulders.

'Errrrm... well... errrrm...' Terry hesitated as he stumbled for an answer. The class sat in a state of stone-cold silence as they listened on.

'Come now Terry, stop being so bashful. It really doesn't become you,' Miss Wells continued.

'Please allow me to step in,' the dry-cleaner man spoke up and as all eyes fell upon him, the only sound heard was Terry taking a deep gulp in order to stop his heart from bursting out of his mouth. 'Earlier this morning, I was looking out from my shop and I spotted an elderly gentleman wondering along the street in his pyjamas in the snow, who I recognised as my old Headmaster, Mr. Miller from this school, from many many years ago. By the time I had the chance to lock up my shop and check on the him, I saw this young boy.' The man pointed directly at Terry and continued, 'I now know him to be Terry Ruddock, and he was holding the man's hand and safely walking him home. I visited the Millers and have since learned, that Mr. James Miller has been struggling with his memory and could not recall his home address.' Terry stood motionless and tried to understand what was going on. The dry-cleaner man pointed at Terry again as he continued his story. 'This young boy had the genius idea to follow Mr. Miller's footprints in the snow in order to get the lost man safely home in quick time. It was a life-saving decision. During the time he was missing, his wife contacted the police. And now, allow me to pass you over to Police Sergeant Jenkins.' The dry-cleaner man finished his speech and listened on as the Sergeant prepared to speak. He shuffled on his feet and cleared his throat before addressing the class.

'As you know of late, the bitter cold has chilled each of us to the bone this year and today was no exception. If it wasn't for Terry's quick thinking in following the footprints back home in time, the freezing weather could have had ended the situation with fatal consequences for Mr. Miller.' The entire class gasped a sigh of relief as they tried to catch their breath, before starting to clap at Terry's achievement, but the Sergeant held his hand up and stopped all the applause. His heart was still pounding but Terry was still unsure of what was going on. The policeman began to speak as silence fell again throughout the class. 'Whilst I was with Mrs. Miller, a neighbour reported that they saw a young boy struggling to help an elderly resident cross the road; which was covered in a layer of fresh, slippery and very dangerous snow. I spoke with several other nearby neighbours in the street, until surprisingly, I found the report to be true. The resident was Mrs. Violet Wilson and she told me how she had been abandoned by a very rude taxi driver. Terry Ruddock, the young boy in question, offered to help take Mrs. Wilson and her heavy load of shopping across the road safely. She concluded by telling me, that he was probably the most charming young man she had ever had the pleasure of meeting.' All eyes fell on Terry again, some even in disbelief. When the applause started, Sergeant Jenkins stopped it yet again with his raised hand and a gentle shake of his head. 'We spoke with the fire brigade this morning and they informed us that a young boy by the name of Terry from a local school saved a call out due to a mother and her distressed child wanting to rescue their pet kitten who had become trapped in a tree top.' The entire class stared at Terry until a hidden shout echoed throughout the room.

'Hey! You're the hero of our class, Terry!' Most of the children turned around and looked at Dexter, but he kept his actions discrete.

'Three cheers for Terry!' Ivy called out, 'Hip hop!'

'Hooray! Hooray! Hooray!' The rest of the class cheered before breaking out into the loudest applause Terry had ever heard in his life. He turned to his right to face Miss Lawford, Miss Wells and Sergeant Jenkins, who were now clapping along just as hard. On his left, the dry-cleaner man and Miss Goode, who mouthed the words to Terry 'I'm sorry I didn't believe you,' also clapped and cheered along. As the applause calmed down, Miss Wells started her speech.

'Today Terry, we would like to award you with the school's first ever medal and certificate for your generosity and kindness in helping others without question. You are our first Hero of the Year!' The words had a magical quality to them, and Terry cherished each one of them. It left him with a special feeling that was more precious than anything he had ever known or felt before.

'Miss Wells?' Terry raised his hand. The class fell silent again.

'Yes?'

'Mrs. Wilson gave me a reward of twenty-pounds for helping her. I would like to share it with the class at the café for mince pies if that's okay?'

Miss Wells felt the pleading glare of the entire class fall upon her and it nearly knocked her off balance. She took a second to compose and reposition herself before speaking.

'Well, it's almost Christmas and I know they have fantastic mince pies at the café. Of course, you can, we'll head over there this afternoon,' she announced. It was another chance for the excited class to roar with joy and they did not hesitate.

– CHAPTER TWENTY-THREE –

'your tree changed because of the good you were doing'

Later that afternoon, Miss Wells stuck to her word and led the class along with Miss Lawford over to the Crossroads Café which was next door to the dry-cleaners. The children huddled into the café and crowded around the tables as they sat down. The entire class ordered their mince pies and the big-hearted café owner even gave away a special treat of hot chocolate with every pie. As the pies were served, the children sipped on their drinks and played name games with Miss Lawford.

Meanwhile, Terry saved the seat next to himself for Dexter, who gladly sat next to him in order to have a private word.

'I wanted to say sorry to you, for what I said. You know, that you were like that horrible twisty tree. But everything makes sense now, you are exactly like it,' said Dexter. Terry looked shocked at what his friend had just said.

'I thought you said, I wasn't like it.' Terry tried to defend himself.

'Your tree has changed, Terry. That's why we were late coming back. It started to grow and flower in front of our own eyes and it had fantastic colourful lights bursting around it.' Dexter revealed.

'But how?' Terry asked.

'It happened while we were there this morning. But you were here, rescuing the kitten, helping the old lady and caring for the old man in pyjamas. Your tree changed because of the good and kind things that you were doing here. You have changed. As we left, the reporters were still there, and they were saying that it's the most spectacular tree in Peckham Rye Park. You'll probably see it on the television tonight.' Dexter spoke with an excited tone in his voice. 'I bet you're not on the flip-reversed anymore either.' Before Terry could answer a voice interrupted the two boys.

'Errrrm, excuse me, young men. Are you two having a private party?' Miss Wells called out from her table. 'We've just come up with a new song for Christmas.' A cheer erupted as Terry smiled and Miss Wells started to sing with the rest of the class.

'We wish you a Terry Christmas! We wish you a Terry Christmas, you're a hero for the New Year!' Amongst the singing and cheering, Ivy sneaked through the crowd and squeezed in and sat next to Terry. She leaned in and spoke discreetly.

'I just wanted to let you know about your tree.'

'Oh, it's okay, I already know, Dexter just…' Terry tried to explain but Ivy was unstoppable.

'Well, I spoke to my grandfather last week about your tree.' Ivy looked over both her shoulders to check if anyone was listening to her before continuing. 'He's mad on gardening stuff and really knows his flowers and trees.' Ivy explained.

'Okay?' Terry listened on, unsure of what she was saying.

'He advised me to care for your tree more than the rest. He said it was in the same earth as the others around it and so it just needed a little more of a chance to grow.'

'Okay.' Terry nodded at Ivy's revelation.

'So, I went back with my grandfather in the evenings this week and watered it. He used a garden fork to 'encourage the earth to breathe and protect' your tree. I don't know what that means but as I said, he's mad about gardening stuff and knows his gardens.'

'Okay?' Terry looked on at Ivy.

'So, I'm just saying,' she tapped her nose and gave a little wink.

'Okay… thank you and thanks to your grandad too,' said Terry.

'That's alright. It's a relief really. I thought the police had come in for me, you know for watering the tree every night. Anyway, you're welcome and don't mention it,' Ivy said before moving off and heading for her second helping of hot chocolate.

– CHAPTER TWENTY-FOUR –

'mostly, I also wanted to say sorry, to you'

Amongst the festive cheers in the café, Terry managed to spot the dry-cleaner man outside speaking with a truck driver. Terry politely asked for another hot chocolate and pie and discreetly took it outside to the dry-cleaner man.

'Hello, Mr. Dry-Cleaner Man. I thought you might like these to help keep you warm out here,' Terry said as he handed him a mince pie and hot chocolate.

'Well, thank you very much. That's very kind of you, I'd love them,' he replied.

'Mostly, I also wanted to say sorry, to you.' Terry looked on extremely embarrassed.

'That's okay. Don't worry about it.'

'But you don't know why I'm saying sorry,' Terry pointed out.

'Well, I assume it's for taking *The Book of Names.*'

'How do you know that?' Terry asked.

'I have a security camera in the shop. I watched it back and saw you run in and take *The Book*. Well, what I mean to say is… I saw you come in and borrow it.' The dry-cleaner man smiled at Terry.

'But borrowing means, it gets returned.' Terry gulped. 'I'm sorry, I don't have it anymore to return it to you,' he confessed.

'I think you found your name on the flip-reversed and so... somehow, ended up without it. Am I right?' the dry-cleaner man asked. Terry kept his head down and just nodded back in silence and shame.

'It's lucky then that I still have the original,' revealed the dry-clean man.

'What? How?' Terry felt a sudden relief.

'With something that's so important and precious, there has to always be a copy and an original.'

'That's brilliant!' Terry beamed from ear to ear.

'Well, imagine if I didn't have *The Book of Names* to give back with the Santa Suit. It would be like a cold afternoon... without hot chocolate.' And on that note, the dry-cleaner man sipped on his hot chocolate and took a bite out of his mince pie. 'Thank you for these by the way, mmm... they're so delicious,' he said. 'Oh, there is one thing you can do for me if that's okay,' he asked.

'Yes, okay, anything,' Terry replied. The dry-cleaner man couldn't speak for a moment as he had just taken another bite out of his tasty mince pie. He indicated for Terry to wait right there and he ran off into the shop only to return with a bag tucked under his arm. He ate the last of the pie and 'mmmd' as he returned, whilst rubbing his hands together and cleaning off the crumbs from his fingertips.

'My hands are a little sticky. Please could you take this bag to the driver in that truck.'

'What is it?' Terry asked. The dry-cleaner man opened the bag for Terry to peek inside.

'Is that... what I think it is?' Terry cautiously asked.

'Yes. It's the original and I promise you that the name Terry Ruddock does not appear on the flip-reversed.' The dry-cleaner man said with a reassuring smile. Terry carefully took the bag and slowly walked over to the truck. The door opened, and he was greeted by the driver who could only be described as a slightly overweight man with a full and fluffy white beard.

'Is that for me?' The driver asked with a cheery tone in his voice. Terry stood motionless staring at the driver before he could only nod back. 'Thank you very much,' he said. Terry placed the bag onto the seat next to the driver and as he did so, he noticed the dry-cleaned Santa Suit hanging behind the front seat. He was left even more stunned when the driver handed him a bunch of wild grasses and bendy stems with berries.

'Is that for me?' an unfamiliar voice trickled out of Terry's mouth.

'Yes, well kind of. I wonder if you can push it through the flap in the side of the truck. He's been so well behaved, it's just a little treat. I'd do it myself, but I think it would attract more attention and cause a bit of a commotion if I got out.' Terry couldn't speak. He closed the door and stepped to the side of the vehicle. He flicked a protective shutter and a flap revealed an opening in the side of the truck. Terry pushed the grass and twisted the stems through the hatch, until he felt them gently taken from his fingertips. The gentle sound of crunching echoed through the hole and curiosity tempted Terry to take a closer look into the back of the truck. He squinted with one eye and stepped closer to the flap with his open eye and peered in. Several berries had snapped off and dropped into the truck and rolled like ruby coloured marbles across the floor. Terry saw the cloven hooves of an animal standing inside and it caused him to reel away until he felt brave enough to take a second inspection. He recognised the head of a reindeer lower its mouth and lick up the loose berries one by one. It pulled away and continued crunching happily on the special treat that had just been delivered through the flap. It was an unexpected sight that caused Terry to stumble back in disbelief. He looked back across to the dry-cleaner man for confirmation, but he placed his finger to his lips and sent Terry a knowing wink before walking back into his shop and calling out.

'Remember! Keep off the flip-reversed!' He gave Terry a thumbs-up and closed the door behind him.

After school, Terry and Ray both headed to Peckham Rye Park to visit the Fairy Tale Forest. They stood motionless staring at the newly flowered tree. Terry could see his name within the small star bursts that popped around its branches and realised all what he had been told was true. His tree had blossomed beautifully. Although it was the same tree it had now surely flourished and began to bloom into something of a wonder. Hidden amongst his name were small flared eruptions of light that revealed the words: 'Caring', 'Kind' and 'Generous'. The words had also changed, and Terry could feel a difference within himself. He felt good and he felt nice and he felt happy about himself and it was a feeling worth enjoying and one that he would always want to keep.

– CHAPTER TWENTY-FIVE –

'it's going to be a Terry Christmas'

The next morning, Terry was awoken by Connor. He had snuck back into the bedroom and was struggling to discretely drag a heavy looking bag behind himself. The noise caused Terry to turn in his sleep and he shuffled himself out of sight and under the covers.

'Wakey, wakey sleeping beauty! Connor called out.

'Hey, there's no school today, leave me alone.' Terry responded from the depths of his slumber as he cocooned himself deeper into his duvet. Connor stepped up onto the end of the bed.

'The postman gave me this bag, Connor announced. 'He said all the cards in it are for a Mr. Terry Ruddock. So, here you are, Mr. Terry Ruddock.' Connor leant over Terry and tipped the bag over his younger brother. Unknown to Terry, Police Sergeant Jenkins had also contacted the local newspaper and informed them about 'the heroic actions of a local boy from a local school'. The extra attention left many residents feeling an overwhelming sense of pride in their neighbourhood for his actions and so they had also sent Terry well-wishes for the Christmas holidays. The postbag also contained a box full of cards for Terry from everyone at Belham Primary School. He couldn't stop the gentle smile which grew across his young face under the covers as over a hundred cards poured down onto his bed. Terry realised there and then that it always felt better to be kind, instead of finding yourself on the pages of the flip-reversed. He also knew this year was going to be a Terry Christmas!

The End.

These next two blank pages are strictly for children only.

Keep off those pages, adults!

Please feel free to write or draw any of your thoughts about this story or any other ideas that pop into your marvelous minds in the space below:

It is a small space – but it's yours. And just like you, all stories and ideas will grow.

This blank page is strictly for children only.

Keep off this page adults!

This blank page is strictly for children only.

Keep off this page adults!

The following questions were found by random searches over the internet and I give full credit and praise to all the genius minds who suggested that these questions be asked, whoever you are. I wish I had been asked them.

Fun questions to ask children when they are busy having a magical time in childhood.

What made you smile today?

Pretend you are a chef and tell me about your restaurant.

What food would you serve?

Can you tell me an example of kindness you saw / showed throughout today?

What did you do that was creative?

Tell me something that you know today that you didn't know yesterday.

Did you like your lunch?

What do you like daydreaming about?

What was the hardest rule for you to follow today?

Do you have any inventions in your brain?

What made your teacher smile / frown today?

If your family owned a circus, what would each of their shows in the circus be?

Do you like it when other people share with you? Why?

What would your very own treehouse look like?

If you could change one thing about your day, what would you choose?

Who did you sit with at lunch?

What animal would you choose to be, but only for one day?

Imagine you are the best photographer in the world. What three photographs would you take?

If you could switch seats with anyone in your class, who would it be? Why?

Imagine you are a famous explorer, where next, would you go in the world with three friends?

If you opened your own store, what would you sell?

What are some of the best things about nature?

What kind of person were you today?

What question would you like to ask?

Printed in Great Britain
by Amazon